THIS DIARY BELONGS TO:

Trudy Alice 'Blue' Weston

AGE: 12

ADDRESS:

Hillrose Poo,

Hardbake Plains, Australia

Books by Katrina Nannestad

Bungaloo Creek
Red Dirt Diaries
Red Dirt Diaries: Blue about Love
Red Dirt Diaries: Blue's News
The Girl Who Brought Mischief

RED DIRT
Diaries

Blue about Love

Katrina Nannestad

ABC
Books

 The ABC 'Wave' device is a trademark of the
Australian Broadcasting Corporation and is used
under licence by HarperCollins*Publishers* Australia.

First published in Australia in 2012
This edition published in 2014
by HarperCollins*Children's Books*
a division of HarperCollins*Publishers* Australia Pty Limited
ABN 36 009 913 517
harpercollins.com.au

HarperCollins*Publishers*
Level 13, 201 Elizabeth Street, Sydney NSW 2000, Australia
Unit D1, 63 Apollo Drive, Rosedale, Auckland 0632, New Zealand
A 53, Sector 57, Noida, UP, India
77–85 Fulham Palace Road, London W6 8JB, United Kingdom
2 Bloor Street East, 20th floor, Toronto, Ontario M4W 1A8, Canada
195 Broadway, New York NY 10007, USA

National Library of Australia Cataloguing-in-Publication entry:

Nannestad, Katrina, author.
  Blue about love / Katrina Nannestad.
  ISBN: 978 0 7333 3395 8 (pbk.)
  Nannestad, Katrina. Red dirt diaries ; 2.
  For primary school age.
  Teachers—Juvenile fiction.
  Love—Juvenile fiction.
  Farm life—Juvenile fiction.
  Australian Broadcasting Corporation.
A823.4

Cover design by Hazel Lam, HarperCollins Design Studio
Cover illustrations by Katrina Nannestad; background images by
shutterstock.com
Internal design by Priscilla Nielsen
Typeset by Kirby Jones
Printed and bound in Australia by McPherson's Printing Group
The papers used by HarperCollins in the manufacture of this book are
a natural, recyclable product made from wood grown in sustainable
plantation forests. The fibre source and manufacturing processes meet
recognised international environmental standards, and carry certification.

To Bloss, Sniff and Mouse

RED DIRT

Diaries

Blue about Love

Dad   Mum   Peter   Sophie

Mildred

Gunther

Gertrude   Doris

Blue (Me!)   Wes   Fez   Fluffles

November

Tuesday, 14 November

I am twelve years old today — a perfect time to start a new diary. Sophie sent me this notebook with little red hearts on the cover, so I might as well use it. I wouldn't be seen dead writing in it at school! I'll use the maggot-shaped notepad Wes and Fez gave me for more public use.

Had a great day, starting with cream and brown sugar on my porridge for breakfast, and the coolest present ever from Mum and Dad — six duck eggs! They're sitting in a cardboard box, with an electric blanket to keep them at just the right temperature until they hatch. They should be ready in two weeks at the most. I can't wait!!!!

After school, Mum took me, the twin tornadoes Wes and Fez and my friends Matilda Jane Sweeney and Banjo Davies over to Dubbo to the circus. It was amazing — trapeze artists, acrobats, jugglers, lion tamers, knife throwers and the funniest clowns I have ever seen. I haven't laughed so hard since Wes knocked himself unconscious trying to break the Guinness World Record for the largest number of wheelbarrows, forty-four gallon drums and dead sheep to be jumped by a pig and chariot. I was just a bit disappointed that they didn't ask for audience participation. I was busting to see Fez's head shoved into a lion's mouth, or Wes fired from a human cannon — preferably as far as possible in the opposite direction to Hillrose Poo, our beloved farm.

After the circus we went to a café for supper. The jugglers were there having pizza. We went over to say hello and they juggled the salt and pepper shakers and knives and forks while they sang 'Happy Birthday to Blue'. Mat was dead jealous. All she did on her birthday was have a lame make-up party.

What a fantastic day!

I have a feeling that this new year of my life is going to be a great one.

Wednesday, 15 November

What a disaster!

This arrived in the mail today:

Mr James Linley Welsh-Pearson and
Miss Katherine Isobel McKenzie

cordially invite
Robert and Valmai Weston and children
to join them in celebrating the joyous event of
their engagement.

1.00 pm
Wednesday, 27 December
at the Welsh-Pearson family home
Hathaway Homestead
Old Birch Road
Bundanoon

RSVP 11 December

What on earth is Miss McKenzie thinking?

And who is Mr James Linley Welsh-Pearson?

Why would Miss McKenzie want to get married? She'd have to leave Hardbake Plains. She loves helping Mr Cluff teach the nineteen kids at our school and living with kind, dotty, old Mrs Whittington. She loves coming out to Hillrose Poo for the day and racing the pig chariots or helping out with the shearing. She loves the cockatoos, the muddy dams and the dust. She even loves the eight-year-old twin tornadoes, Wes and Fez!

Why does she want to marry this bloke?

It can't be because she loves *him* ... can it?

Thursday, 16 November

Showed Mat the invitation at school today.

She pulled a matching invitation from her pocket and started jumping up and down, screaming like a maniac! I was horrified that she was actually *excited* at the idea of Miss McKenzie getting married, so *I* started jumping up and down screaming.

Mat screamed and jumped and cried tears of joy, and *I* screamed and jumped and cried tears of grief. Miss McKenzie joined us and screamed and jumped and cried tears of laughter because being in love has obviously turned her brain to mush. We were like clowns in a circus.

Mat suddenly turned into Matilda Jane the Mature — expert on romance, fashion and filing fingernails. She threw herself at Miss McKenzie and blubbered like she'd just been crowned Miss Universe. While she was saying stuff like 'Congratulations-and-I-wish-you-both-every-happiness-in-the-world,' I pulled myself together.

I clenched my teeth and smiled until my face felt like it was going to split and all the freckles were about to pop off. I gave Miss McKenzie a hug. I didn't want her to see how devastated I was, so I wiped my nose and eyes on her lovely curly red hair.

Thank goodness for the duck eggs. Six fluffy ducklings is something exciting to look forward to.

Friday, 17 November

Four fluffy ducklings to look forward to.

Wes and Fez thought it would be fun to introduce Gunther to the eggs before school this morning. Gunther, the meanest pig on earth, did seem quite interested, snuffling around in an odd sort of way. He was, however, far more excited at the sight of Wes's bum as he bent over the cardboard box.

Gunther charged and bit Wes on the left buttock. Wes jumped around crying and clutching his bum in agony. Fez laughed his guts out, so Wes punched Fez in the face. Fez stumbled backwards, tripped over and fell onto the box of eggs …

Four eggs remaining.

Saturday, 18 November

Tennis out at the Sweeneys' all afternoon.

I thought beating Mat six–love might cheer me up a bit, but Mat was too obsessed with THE WEDDING to care.

It turns out that James Welsh-Pearson is a lawyer from Sydney. Miss McKenzie met him at a Scottish ball in the July holidays.

Mat is ecstatic.

'Gavin O'Donnell is going to be a lawyer!' she cried. 'What an amazing coincidence! Miss McKenzie and I could *both* end up married to lawyers … How astonishing!'

The really astonishing thing is how Mat can *still* dream of riding into the sunset on a white stallion with Peter's friend Gavin O'Donnell, when Gavin O'Donnell doesn't even know that she exists!

Sophie sent a tragic email from boarding school. She thinks Miss McKenzie's engagement is THE MOST AWESOME THING IN THE *WHOLE WIDE WORLD*. She can't wait to see the engagement ring and ask Miss McKenzie all about her wedding dress and blah, blah, blah. She'd emailed a 5000-word essay on the joys of marriage, but I deleted it after reading the first few lines.

Sophie is such a traitor. Not only do she and Peter continue to return to boarding school every term, despite the fact that I beg them to run away home, now she is acting like Miss McKenzie is doing something great.

Why is everyone so excited about this wedding? It's obviously an embarrassing mistake.

Wes and Fez have stolen the curtain rod from my bedroom, so I have nothing to cover my windows. Gerty, Doris and Mildred, the three greediest pigs in the universe, are standing outside right now with their snouts pressed against the glass. I think they're hoping I'll pass some of my chocolate bickies out to them. There's pig snot everywhere.

Sunday, 19 November

Wes and Fez used my curtain rod as a double trapeze bar today. They tied a rope to each end and hung it off the peppercorn tree. They sat side by side on the bar and swung out. The plan was to leap off together, bounce on the trampoline, fly into the air for a synchronised somersault and land feet first on the grass near the clothesline.

Unfortunately, the trapeze bar bent. By the time they reached the trampoline, Wes was dangling upside down with Fez sitting on top of him. They couldn't jump off, so they swung backwards into the tree trunk where Wes grazed the side of his face and Fez fell into the fork of the tree, grazing half his bum off.

It was fantastic!

Gunther is acting very oddly around the duck eggs. I thought he was going to eat them but he stands in front of the box as if he's guarding it. Every time I get close, his hair stands on end and his nostrils flare.

I got Fez to come and help but every time *he* went near, Gunther bared his teeth and snarled. Sort of like a starving, rabid Rottweiler guarding its bone, only more vicious.

We just had to leave him there in the end.

Dear God, please keep my ducklings safe.

And please don't let Miss McKenzie marry this bloke from Sydney.

Monday, 20 November

Phew! All four eggs are still there!!

Gunther is still there too. But at least he hasn't eaten the eggs.

WHAT IS THAT CRAZY PIG DOING??????

Wes and Fez started an acrobatic craze at school today. They're really quite good at doing cartwheels and inspired a whole heap of kids to start spinning across the playground. Tom Gillies did ten cartwheels in a row until he flipped through the wing of the aeroplane Harry Wilson is building to fly to Greenland. Harry was furious and hit Tom over the head with his flying goggles.

Davo Hartley cartwheeled into Lynette Sweeney and made her cry. Nick Farrel loves Lynette. He was furious so he hit Davo over the head with a plastic cricket bat.

Ben Simpson cartwheeled straight into Sam Wotherspoon's compost heap. Sam was furious about Ben squashing his worms so he hit him over the head with a large zucchini from his vegie patch.

What an awesome lunch time — every bit as funny as watching the clowns at the circus.

Tuesday, 21 November

Count down till harvest!

After all those years of dust and dirt and dying sheep, we're surrounded by beautiful, golden-brown wheat. It spreads out as far as the eye can see, and flows and ripples like water on a lake when there's a breeze. Hillrose Poo has to be the most beautiful place on earth.

We hardly see Dad these days; he's so busy getting the machinery and silos ready. But when we do, he's smiling, whistling and talking about bumper crops.

Wes and Fez started teaching everyone flips at school today. It was going just fine until they talked Lynette into trying a flip off the picnic table. Lynette climbed up on the table, slipped on Sarah Love's salami sandwich and fell on her head with a crack.

Sarah was devastated. She ran to Miss McKenzie, bawling and waving her squished sandwich in the air.

Nick Farrel was really mad that his beloved Lynette was hurt so he hit Wes over the head with a plastic cricket bat.

Mr Cluff got mad and banned acrobatics.

Forever!

Don't know what *his* problem is. He doesn't usually get flustered about anything — not even the really stupid stuff Wes and Fez get up to.

Banjo is loving Wes and Fez's whole circus craze. He's been jotting down verses on his notepad all day. I heard him muttering:

Lynette slipped over on Sarah's salami,
Came crashing down like a giant tsunami.

I suggested he add:

Nick belted Wes over the head,
Blue was hoping that Wes was dead.

But he doesn't like other people interfering in his writing.

Still avoiding Miss McKenzie. I can't stand the idea of her marrying this bloke from Sydney. I don't want to offend her by telling her what a stupid, foolish thing she's going to do, but I can't lie, can I? That would be dishonest.

Wednesday, 22 November

I'm going to be a bridesmaid.

Mat, Lynette and me.

Long, pink shiny dresses and flowers in our hair.

Leading Miss McKenzie down the aisle to disaster.

I think I'm going to puke.

Thursday, 23 November

Gunther is refusing to eat. Pigs never refuse to eat — unless they're emotionally unstable ... or dead.

He won't leave the duck eggs and he won't let me anywhere near them. All I can do is make sure the electric blanket stays on to keep the eggs warm. Don't know why I bother. He'll probably eat the poor little things when they hatch.

Still avoiding Miss McKenzie. I will *not* pretend that this wedding is a good idea. And I absolutely *refuse* to be a bridesmaid.

Friday, 24 November

Told Miss McKenzie how excited and honoured I am to be her bridesmaid.

She was really happy and gave my hand a squeeze, so I told her how delighted I am that she is getting married.

I'm such a BIG, FAT LIAR.

I was so mad at myself that I came home and shoved Gunther in the guts to get him away from my duck eggs. It didn't work. Gunther just squealed and bit me. Mum had to take me over to the Sweeneys' for a tetanus needle and six stitches in my leg. I told Mr Sweeney we were lucky to have a local vet who could patch up humans as well as animals. Mr Sweeney said I was lucky Gunther didn't bite down harder or I'd be on my way to Dubbo to see a real doctor, or maybe even a surgeon.

Mat is insanely excited about the whole wedding–bridesmaid thing. I was speechless, so I just sat on the end of her bed and listened to her gush and sigh over how romantic and beautiful it will all be, as she put my red hair in a French knot and arranged violets from their garden into a bridesmaid's bouquet. The pain from Gunther's attack was nothing compared to the pain who was doing my hair while drivelling on about true love!

Saturday, 25 November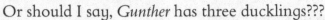

I have three ducklings!

Or should I say, *Gunther* has three ducklings???

They hatched this morning and seem to have decided that Gunther is their mother. They are snuggled between his front legs, tucked under his fat, piggy jowls. I suppose it's nice and warm there. He is uncharacteristically gentle with them and has been making quiet little murmuring sounds all day.

I desperately want to play with the ducklings. They are *my* birthday present after all, but Gunther won't let me near them.

At least I managed to rescue the last egg and hide it in my bedroom. It's wrapped up in my winter pyjamas and the electric blanket. Maybe it will still hatch and I can have one duckling all to myself.

Wes and Fez have given up cartwheeling and flips.

'They're too dangerous, Blue,' Wes said.

'Yeah, someone might get hurt,' Fez said.

So they started doing circus stunts on the trampoline this afternoon instead!

'We're the Flying Ferals!' they cried.

'It's all about how far you can fly through the air, Blue!' cried Wes.

'The further the better, Blue!' cried Fez.

Fez must have been very satisfied because he jumped from the laundry roof onto the trampoline, then flew at least five metres through the air before he landed in a patch of stinging nettles.

Sunday, 26 November

I have a duckling!

Her name is Petal. She is yellow and fluffy and fits snugly inside my shirt pocket. She is already in love with me and makes sweet little *peep-peep-peep* noises when I hold her up to my face.

Better still, every time Wes or Fez hold her, she poos on their hand.

I think we are going to have a wonderful relationship.

Gunther already has a wonderful, although bizarre, relationship with the other three ducklings. They follow him back and forth along the veranda and if one is lagging behind, he stops and makes a soft grunt. When it catches up, he bows his head to the ground for a duckling kiss — a nibble on the snout followed by cute little *peep-peep-peep* sounds.

I can't believe how tender Gunther is. Gunther, who has been responsible for more tetanus injections, stitches and dressings than all the rusty barbed wire and corrugated iron this side of the Black Stump!

He is totally transformed. He is just so, so gentle.

Monday, 27 November

Gunther ripped the ear off one of the farm dogs this afternoon.

Burley got off his leash and ran onto the veranda. The ducklings got a fright and scattered but Burley rounded one up near the firewood box.

Gunther turned into a ferocious mother lioness defending her cubs. He leapt on top of Burley, pinning him to the ground and savaging his ear. Poor mutt ran down the driveway yelping, tail between his legs, while Gunther stood on the edge of the veranda squealing and frothing at the mouth. Then, like changing the channel on the TV, he turned around to his ducklings and made gentle, loving grunts until they waddled back to him and nibbled at his snout. Amazing!

Fez doesn't know how to deal with the whole mother-duck side of Gunther. I think he's ashamed of him. He called him a sissy-pink-pants and stormed off to find Wes to do some pig chariot racing with Doris and Mildred.

Tuesday, 28 November

Thank goodness for Matilda Jane the Mature. If I didn't have her to copy, I wouldn't know *how* to behave around Miss McKenzie. Mum and Dad are always telling me to be myself and act naturally. But if I did what comes naturally at the moment, I'd be shaking Miss McKenzie by the shoulders and screaming at her to forget James Welsh-Pearson and stay at Hardbake Plains where she belongs.

Somehow, I don't think that's what she wants to hear right now.

So today, when Mat sighed at Miss McKenzie and clutched her chest as though her heart was about to burst, I really paid attention so I can do it myself some time. When she asked Miss McKenzie detailed questions about fabrics and veils and petticoats and hosiery, I jotted the words down in my maggot notepad. I researched the words after school so I'll be ready to use them tomorrow if I need to. It turns out, by the way, that *hosiery* is not for irrigating vegie patches or filling the troughs up with water. It's the mature word for stockings!

After just one day of close observation, I have a bank of five actions that I can use when talking to Miss McKenzie about her engagement and wedding:

- The chest clutch
- Tucking hair behind ears while talking enthusiastically about wedding dresses
- Crossing one foot over the other and swaying from side to side while asking a question about honeymoons
- Fluttering eyelashes (especially helpful when I have tuned out and can't give an intelligent answer)
- Rolling eyes backwards in head while fanning face rapidly with both hands (save for very emotional moments, like a closer look at the enormous ruby and diamond engagement ring)

Who would ever have thought that being excited for the joy in someone's life could be such hard work????

Mum interrupted my eyelash fluttering practice this evening to let me know that James Welsh-Pearson is coming to stay with us on the weekend!!!

I clutched my chest, swayed from side to side and rolled my eyes back into my head.

'Hosiery … carnations … rubies … taffeta …' I sighed and swooned onto my bed.

Mum left my room laughing.

Petal pooped on my bedspread.

I'm with Petal on this one.

Wednesday, 29 November

Dad started harvesting today. Don't suppose we'll see too much of him before Christmas. He sure was happy when he headed off this morning, whistling and making up silly songs about bumper crops.

'Nothing like a good harvest, Blue,' he said.

He took a fistful of wheat grain out of his pocket and poured it into my hand. He said it was a bit of gold to remind me why the Westons stick with the red dirt no matter how tough the going gets.

Petal came to school with me today. She sat in a shoebox full of tissues on my desk. Lynette and Sarah were dead jealous of the way Petal talks softly and nibbles my cheek. Even Mat thinks she's cute.

At lunch time, Lucy Ferris had just filled a bowl of water for her rabbits when Petal popped up onto the edge and jumped in. She swam round and round in the tiny dish and looked like she was in heaven.

Mr Cluff said she took to it like a duck to water! Ha, ha, ha!

Miss McKenzie wanted me to bring Petal into the little kids' classroom for Show and Share after lunch, but I pretended it was her nap time.

I just don't know what to say to Miss McKenzie any more. I can't go on avoiding her forever, though, can I?

Thursday, 30 November

Wes didn't come to school today. Just before we were meant to leave, he ran in crying. His arm was bleeding all over the kitchen floor.

Fez ran in after him, carrying three steak knives, yelling, 'It's Wes's fault, Mummy! He was a coward! You're not meant to move halfway through a knife-throwing performance!'

He's right, you know. The lady at the circus didn't duck when Rasmov the Great threw knives at her. She didn't even blink.

Petal is crazy about water. Today she spent our entire maths lesson swimming around in an ice-cream container full of water on my desk. She stopped every three or four circuits to *peep* happily at me, as though she wanted to share her joy.

And then I realised — Miss McKenzie wants to share *her* joy.

I must try harder with this whole wedding thing.

December

Friday, 1 December

Looked at material samples with Mat and Miss McKenzie for THIRTY WHOLE MINUTES at lunch time today. It was TORTURE!

I tried really hard to say things that would make Miss McKenzie think I cared. I tucked my hair behind my ears and asked her what colour she thought would look best for our bridesmaids' dresses. Mat and Miss McKenzie both stared at me oddly. That's when I noticed that all *eleven* samples were pink …

So I giggled and clutched my chest and fluttered my eyelids. I think I might have even said 'hosiery' a few times. I crossed my legs and swayed from side to side and rolled my eyes back into my head like I'd seen Mat do. Unfortunately, I lost my balance and fell over sideways, banging my head on the edge of the tank stand.

The next thing I remember is Mum arriving to pick me up. Banjo was standing over me with his notepad, mumbling, 'Blue … twit … fell … head hit.' That boy has to make a poem of everything!

I'm in bed with Petal and Fluffles as I write this. Petal is eating the coconut from the lamington Mum brought in for me. Fluffles is flicking her tail from side to side. I think she would like to be eating Petal.

I must practise fluttering my eyelids and rolling my eyes back in my head so that I can do it without getting dizzy.

HOW AM I EVER GOING TO GET THROUGH THIS WHOLE WEDDING THING?

9 pm

Good grief! Mum just came in to kiss me goodnight and reminded me that James Welsh-Pearson is arriving tomorrow. I think I'm going to be sick and it has nothing to do with the lump the size of a golf ball sticking out the side of my forehead.

Saturday, 2 December

Poor James Welsh-Pearson.

Miss McKenzie arrived at eleven, looking beautiful as ever. She was wearing a white dress covered in big red roses. Her hair looked a bit odd — sort of tidy, as though she'd tried to make it straight — but the carroty curls were soon frizzing out all over the place. A quick race in a pig chariot pulled by Doris saw to that.

Just after midday, Wes and Fez cheered from the top of the chook shed as James Welsh-Pearson drove down the driveway. Fez leapt from the chook shed roof onto the trampoline and flew through the air, landing feet first on the dirt like a real pro. Wes leapt down from the chook shed roof onto the trampoline and flew through the air until he hit the peppercorn tree face first. He staggered over to the driveway.

Our welcoming committee was all there — Doris, Mildred and Gertrude, the three fattest sows on earth, Gunther with his three ducklings, Fez grinning stupidly, Wes bawling his eyes out with blood gushing from his nose, Mum in her apron, Dad in his dusty work clothes just in from the paddocks, me practising my fake welcome-and-congratulations-on-your-engagement smile, Petal peeping out of my pocket, and Miss McKenzie looking like she was about to open the best Christmas present ever.

A red Ferrari screeched to a halt, sending gravel flying towards Gunther's ducklings. Gunther was furious.

James Welsh-Pearson stepped out of the car, holding an enormous bunch of red roses. Gunther squealed and lunged forward, frothing at the mouth. He latched onto James's shin and chomped down. The red roses flew into the air and landed on Doris's back. The thorns must have given her a terrible fright because she spun around and bit the first thing she found, which happened to be the Ferrari's front tyre. It exploded like a gunshot and sent a flock of cockatoos screeching overhead, splattering the car with fresh white parrot droppings. Gunther started to growl and shake James's leg from side to side.

Meanwhile, Gertrude sneaked into the car, lured by the smell of food. She found a large box of chocolates which she ripped open and scoffed, then went on to eat the leather upholstery from the passenger seat.

James let out a cry of agony — I'm not sure whether it was pain from the deep gash on his leg, or horror at what was happening to his car.

Thankfully Fez stopped laughing long enough to yell, 'Gunther! Dinner time!'

Gunther let go of the leg and sprinted around to the back door, where he gets fed. Gertrude leapt from the car, knocking James to the ground, and trotted after Gunther, followed by Doris, Mildred, the three ducklings and Wes, who was bawling and dripping blood.

Mum and Dad helped James hobble into the house. Miss McKenzie followed behind looking a bit dazed.

Of course, Mr Sweeney, local vet and pretend doctor, had to be called. But even *he* couldn't mend poor James's savaged leg. Dad and Miss McKenzie had to drive him to Dubbo, where he's spending the night in hospital.

Sunday, 3 December

James Leg-Torn-Off has gone back to Sydney on crutches!

His red Ferrari is parked in the shed with the tractor and the hay-baler.

Miss McKenzie is heartbroken. She won't be seeing James again until Christmas. She sat in the kitchen with Mum and cried for TWO HOURS.

I'd never seen Miss McKenzie cry before. I once saw her lip wobble when we thought Mrs Whittington was going to be sent back to the nursing home, but I've never ever seen her cry. She's always smiling and laughing. That's why she's got wrinkles around her eyes when she's only twenty-seven.

I kept wondering what Matilda Jane the Mature would say in this situation. She seems to know an awful lot about boys and romance and all that stuff. Even though she's an airhead, I couldn't help thinking that she would have known the right thing to do here.

I tried fluttering my eyelashes and rolling my eyes, but Miss McKenzie didn't seem to notice.

'Love hurts sometimes,' I said in my most mature voice.

Mum scowled and sent me outside to feed the chooks and get the washing off the line.

Monday, 4 December

I thought I'd be glad when James Leg-Torn-Off left, but Miss McKenzie is miserable. Her eyes looked all red and puffy when she came out for playground duty at lunch time.

Mr Cluff tried to cheer her up with a cup of tea. He even put his arm around her shoulder and gave her a squeeze. She didn't crack a smile, but it *did* seem to cheer Mr Cluff up a bit.

I took Petal over to say hello. She pecked Miss McKenzie's cheek and said, '*Peep-peep-peep,*' so sweetly that I was sure she would smile. But she didn't.

She didn't even smile when Davo ran over the top of Wes on his BMX bike. And that really *was* funny.

Good old Mrs Whittington popped over at lunch time with a steamed golden syrup pudding. She often brings me one as a reward for an essay competition I won two years ago. She thinks it was only last week and keeps forgetting that she has already made me lots of puddings.

Mrs Whittington took one look at Petal today and said, 'I don't know what the world's coming to, Blue. That's the sickliest looking dog I've ever seen. It all has to do with this dreadful global warming. Before you know what's happened, the cows and sheep will be so small that there won't be enough meat for us to eat and we'll all starve to death. I just hope and pray that I don't live to see the day.'

She walked straight back out the gate and across the road to her house, shaking her head sadly all the way.

She took the pudding with her.

Miss McKenzie looked at me and burst out laughing.

Thank goodness for Mrs Whittington!

Tuesday, 5 December

Petal, Mat and I sat on the steps in the sun, watching Gabby Woodhouse at lunch time. She spent twenty-five minutes trimming one of the shrubs with a pair of scissors. We thought she'd taken a sudden interest in gardening, but when she finished, she held up a mirror, leant over the shrub and asked if it wanted a bit of hairspray to keep things in place.

We nearly died laughing. Mat laughed so hard she snorted a bit of snot out her nose. She was *so* embarrassed!

What would Gavin O'Donnell think????

The Flying Ferals started working on their latest acrobatic trick when we got home. Fez jumped up and down on the trampoline, getting higher and higher. When Wes ran past, Fez was going to do a somersault in the air and land on Wes's shoulders.

Yeah, right.

Fez did *one and a half* somersaults in the air, landed on a rock and split his forehead open. Wes kept running while he was looking back at Fez and ran into the veranda post. He split the back of his head open.

Mr Sweeney came over with his vet's bag and gave Wes five stitches and Fez three stitches. Fez was bawling his eyes out.

Mum thought he was scared of the tetanus needle, but it turns out he was jealous that Wes got more stitches than him.

Wednesday, 6 December

Miss McKenzie has given me, Mat and Lynette a bridesmaid's scrapbook each. It has pictures of different dresses and little squares of pink fabric stuck all over the place.

Mat is ecstatic. I've never seen her eyes roll so far back in her head, or her hands work so hard fanning her face. It was such an EMOTIONAL moment.

We're meant to be deciding on which fabric

we like best, but they all look the same to me —
pink and totally gross.

Showed Gerty the scrapbook and she snuffled
sadly at it. She seemed quite upset at the idea of
me wearing a dress that would make me look
like a ball of fairy floss. Then
again, she might have been
upset that I was showing her
pieces of fabric rather than
a slice of cake or a crumpet
with butter and honey. You
never can tell with pigs.

Thursday, 7 December

Fez was attacked this morning. He went out the
back door to get his school shoes, and Gunther's
ducklings popped out of nowhere. They charged
like a mini light horse brigade and pecked his
bare feet over and over again.

Fez danced around, half-laughing, half-crying,
because it tickled so much. Gunther lay on the
veranda, watching out of the corner of his eyes.

When Fez ran inside, the ducklings
waddled back to Gunther and lay down
between his front legs.

I think Gunther *smirked*!!!!

How cool is that? Ducklings trained to kill Wes and Fez.

Gunther is my hero.

I was going to pat him on the head, but when I stepped forwards, he bared his teeth and snarled at me like a dog. That pig is so out of control.

Friday, 8 December

Lucy, Banjo and I spent lunch time playing with Lucy's baby rabbits and Petal. Mat sat on the grass nearby and pretended to be totally unimpressed.

The baby bunnies were frolicking around, so Petal started jumping like a baby bunny. It was so incredibly cute that Mat couldn't resist. She just had to join in and play with us.

We were having so much fun until Mat went and spoiled it all by talking about the wedding.

'It's so romantic,' she sighed. 'Miss McKenzie is going to be so happy … James and Katherine Welsh-Pearson … It sounds so *perfect*.'

She rolled her eyes and fluttered her eyelids … and she didn't even seem to get dizzy!

'She's so, so lucky. James will take her away from all this.' Mat made a dramatic sweeping movement with her arm that took in the whole playground.

I looked around. The little kids were giggling at the rude body parts they were making in the sandpit. Davo and Gary were screaming around on their BMX bikes trying to run Wes and Fez down. Mr Cluff and Harry were smiling proudly at the propeller they had just attached to Harry's aeroplane. Gabby Woodhouse was talking excitedly to the lavender she was giving a haircut. Sam Wotherspoon was giving Sarah Love a hug of appreciation for the worm she had just given him for his compost heap. And Miss McKenzie was sitting on the veranda steps, hugging a cup of tea in her hands and laughing at Gary and Nick's latest dance, the Christmas fling.

WHY ON EARTH WOULD SHE WANT TO LEAVE ALL THIS????

Saturday, 9 December

Drove out on the harvester with Dad this morning. When I got back to the house, Petal went crazy. She rubbed her head all over my cheeks and nibbled my ears. Every time I put her down on the floor she quacked like a lunatic until I picked her up again.

Mum said Petal had been sulking since I went out with Dad. She'd stood at the back door and quacked for nearly an hour, then waddled into my room, flopped down on my sheepskin rug and moaned. She's not used to being left behind. Poor little darling.

Gertrude went feral this evening.

When Miss McKenzie first came from Scotland to Hardbake Plains, she lived at Hillrose Poo for a while, in our shearers' cottage. It was lovely, except that she used to play the bagpipes *every single day*. They sounded dreadful — like a hundred cats being sat on by a bellowing bull. But Gertrude, crazy pig, loved it. She became a full-on addict.

Ever since Miss McKenzie and her bagpipes left Hillrose Poo to live with Mrs Whittington, we've had to play a CD of Scottish bagpipe music every morning and night. If we forget, Gerty gets agitated and paces up and down the veranda squealing, or gets depressed and runs away from home. Last time we went away overnight, she ended up at Ned Murphy's house,

34

three farms away. So now we just play the bagpipes CD as part of our daily routine, like feeding the dogs or collecting the eggs.

Tonight, though, Wes and Fez thought Gerty might like a change. They played their old *Sesame Street* CD. Instead of the bagpipes belching out across the plains, Cookie Monster sang the song 'C is for Cookie'.

It turns out that Gerty *didn't* want a change. She was furious. She squealed and head-butted Mum as she walked out onto the veranda. Mum ended up in the firewood box with splinters in all sorts of awkward places. She was not impressed.

Sunday, 10 December

Found the *Sesame Street* CD in the scrap bucket this morning. Hope the chooks like it better than Gerty did.

Sat up the back of Mass with Petal in my lap. I could hardly leave her home alone after yesterday.

It's great in the back row. You get to spy on everyone.

Ned Murphy's mum ate three packets of jelly babies during Mass.

Mr Sweeney slept through Father O'Malley's sermon.

Mum spent a big part of Mass praying on her knees. Splinters can be a bummer.

Ben Simpson tore a page out of his prayer book and made a paper crane. And I'm still not sure which is more shocking — the fact that Ben tore the prayer book, or that he knows how to make a delicate piece of origami.

Gabby Woodhouse sat behind Mat. Mat never kneels during prayers. She doesn't want to crease the front of her skirt. Gabby *always* kneels during prayers because sometimes she can get close enough to people's hair to play with it. By the time the prayer was finished she'd put three paperclips, five unicorn stickers and a piece of yellow crepe paper in the ends of Mat's hair. Mat will be livid when she finds out.

I prayed for Miss McKenzie: Dear God, please don't let her make a huge mistake.

Monday, 11 December

This morning while we were waiting down at the front gate, Wes and Fez decided to try tightrope walking on the fence. By the time the bus picked us up, Wes was covered in dust and had a bleeding nose, and Fez was winded. When Fez got his breath back he vomited on Lynette's backpack, so Nick Farrel punched him in the face.

By the time we arrived at school, Wes and Fez *both* had bleeding noses.

Synchronised nose bleeding. Now there's a circus act!

Then, as if they hadn't done enough for one day, Wes and Fez gave Gabby a crew cut at recess. Gabby bawled her eyes out until home time.

Wes and Fez were totally confused.

'Why would she be crying?' asked Fez. 'It looks cool as!'

'I thought she liked crew cuts,' said Wes. 'It's just like the one she gave Lynette last year.'

He does have a point there.

Tuesday, 12 December

It was my turn to drive the old ute to the bus stop this morning. The sun was shining, the birds were singing, the golden wheat swayed gently in the morning air ... and then a galah splattered on the windscreen.

'You drive like a maniac, Blue,' said Wes.

'You make us nervous,' said Fez.

And they meant it! The Flying Ferals think *I'm* dangerous and reckless!

They got out and walked the rest of the way.

When we got to school, Wes and Fez gave Gabby a purple and green tea cosy to cover her crew cut. Gabby burst out crying again. Wes assured her it would look cool and put it on her head to demonstrate. He pulled one of Gabby's ears out the hole for the teapot spout and the other ear out the hole for the teapot handle. He flicked the pom-pom on the top so that it wobbled.

Gabby ran into the toilets and wouldn't come out again.

'That looked so cool,' said Wes.

'Yeah. I wish I'd kept it for myself,' said Fez.

Those boys are insane.

Wednesday, 13 December

Hinted to Mat that Miss McKenzie might be making a mistake marrying James Welsh-Pearson. Her eyes nearly popped out of her head. She couldn't possibly imagine *anything* more exciting than marrying James Welsh-Pearson.

'He's a lawyer and he's rich and he drives a cool car and he lives in the city. It's all so wonderfully perfect and romantic,' she gushed.

Mat's never even *met* the bloke and she thinks he's the most awesome thing in the whole wide universe — apart from Gavin O'Donnell, of course (blush, smirk, simper, eyelash flutter, etc, etc …).

I told her that Miss McKenzie should be staying here in Hardbake Plains where she belongs.

Mat burst out laughing and told me not to be so stupid. Nobody in their right mind would want to stay in Hardbake Plains.

I told her that calling *me* stupid was definitely a case of the pot calling the kettle black. Mat grabbed her bridesmaid's scrapbook and stormed off to gush and sigh and flutter her eyelashes with Miss McKenzie.

It used to be *me* who got on so well with Miss McKenzie. Mat thought she was too uncool with her frizzy hair and freckles and bagpipes and soccer playing. But *now* look at them. They're like Siamese twins joined at the fabric sample!

Everything is all wrong. What am I going to do?

Thursday, 14 December

Wes and Fez both wore tea cosies to school today. Wes had a pink and purple crocheted tea cosy with a big pink pom-pom on top. Fez had an owl-shaped tea cosy with two googly eyes at the front. They looked so stupid.

Gabby thought they were making fun of her and burst out crying *again*.

Gunther didn't like the tea cosies either. When Wes and Fez got home and tried to go in the back door, Gunther stood at the edge of the veranda and snarled at them. The three ducklings stood beside him and peeped angrily. Wes and Fez had to walk around the house and go in through the front door.

Sophie and Peter will be home from boarding school in five days. At long last, they will be back at Hillrose Poo where they belong. And best of all, they'll be home for SEVEN WHOLE WEEKS.

Friday, 15 December

Got Mr Cluff to copy some photos for me so I can make a special birthday present for Mum. He pointed out that I had seven photos of the pigs, three photos of Fluffles and eight photos of sheep, but had forgotten to include any pictures of Wes and Fez. I pointed out that Wes and Fez were, at that moment, running around the playground, wearing tea cosies on their heads, waving Sam's giant zucchinis at Sarah Love and Grace Simpson.

Mr Cluff smiled sympathetically but printed off a school photo of Wes and Fez, just in case I changed my mind.

He also printed off a photo of Miss McKenzie, which he tucked away in his diary. Weird!

Three days until Mum's birthday.

Four days until Sophie and Peter return.

Saturday, 16 December

Mum was driving the grain truck from the paddocks to the silos today, so I was left at home with Wes and Fez. I hid in my room all day so I didn't have to see what they were up to. Started making Mum's birthday present.

Petal pooped on the photo of Wes and Fez. She's so clever.

When I came out of my room to make a milkshake, there was a trail of Band-Aid wrappers through the kitchen and I could see Wes's bicycle hanging off the edge of the trampoline. I hid back in my bedroom with Petal and Fluffles and read for the rest of the day.

Sophie and Peter will be home on Tuesday and I will feel much safer.

Sunday, 17 December

Decorated the Christmas tree today. Mum thought it would be a quiet, safe thing for us to do while she and Dad were away from the house. It ended up covered in red and gold baubles, silver tinsel, little white snowmen and strings of rabbit poo that Wes and Fez had spent all afternoon threading together with needles and cotton. They laughed and laughed as though it was the cleverest thing they had ever done. Actually, it probably *is* the cleverest thing they have ever done, which doesn't say much about the rest of their lives …

Mum freaked when she saw it. She made them take it all off, but the lounge room still smells a bit whiffy.

Only two days until Sophie and Peter are home for the holidays!

Monday, 18 December

Happy birthday, Mum!

Mum loved the scrapbook of her life that I gave her. She flicked through it, smiling at first, then crying a little bit at the photo of Sophie, me, Mum and Granny Parker just before Granny died. She didn't even seem to notice that there wasn't any mention of Wes and Fez in the whole thing. I wish they'd slip *my* mind so easily …

Didn't have a party or anything. Mum and Dad are too busy with the harvesting. Mum said there's no rest for the wicked, but that's not true otherwise Wes and Fez wouldn't sleep a wink.

Mat spent the whole of lunch time making me practise the bridesmaid's walk for Miss McKenzie's wedding. Apparently it's not good enough to just wander up the aisle of the church in front of the bride. You have to do this freaky thing where you step and stop, drag one foot up beside the other, step and stop, drag the other foot up beside the first one, step and stop …

I tried to do it properly, but I got totally tangled up in my own feet. I just kept limping like I was a war veteran with shrapnel embedded in my leg. Mat was furious and said I wasn't taking my bridesmaid duties seriously.

It was all very, very depressing.

At least Sophie and Peter will be home tomorrow.

Tuesday, 19 December

They are home at last!

Mrs O'Donnell dropped them off just after Wes, Fez and I got home on the bus.

I told Gavin that Mat was looking forward to seeing him, and he asked, 'Who?' Mat will be devastated when I tell her.

Wes and Fez celebrated the grand homecoming by teaching Peter their latest stunts on the trampoline. Sophie and I cooked dinner.

When Mum and Dad came in at eight for a break from harvesting, we all sat down together and ate lamb chops, mashed potatoes and peas, and steamed golden syrup pudding with custard made from fresh eggs. It was just perfect.

Mum showed Sophie and Peter the invitation to Miss McKenzie's engagement party. Peter said James Welsh-Pearson sounds like the name of a wrestling manoeuvre. He grabbed Dad in a headlock and pulled his arm back to demonstrate.

Dad's eyes nearly popped out of his head and his shoulder popped out of its socket. Mr Sweeney had to come and pop it back in before Dad could go out on the harvester again. Dad bellowed like a bull getting branded.

Wes and Fez thought it looked as cool as anything. They are in their bedroom right now, wrestling and trying to pull each other's arms out of their sockets.

Sophie, Petal and I are sitting on my bed as I write this. Sophie is looking at my bridesmaid scrapbook. I think she feels a bit left out. I'd gladly swap places with her.

Wednesday, 20 December

Mat made me practise the bridesmaid's walk again today. I got so tangled up in my own feet that I tripped over and sprained my ankle. Now I'm limping like a war veteran *all the time!*

Petal the copy cat limped along behind me for the rest of the day. Mat said my duck can do the bridesmaid's walk better than me.

That was hurtful.

Did the big end-of-year school clean-up after lunch. Found seven dead mice in the store room. They turned up again at home, hanging from our Christmas tree. Mum threw them out the lounge-room window. Doris and Mildred ate them.

Sophie and I spent the evening writing Christmas cards. Sophie has forty-seven cards finished, sealed in envelopes together with thousands of tiny silver stars, ready to hand out.

I didn't get very far. I tore up thirteen cards trying to write the proper words for Miss McKenzie. Somehow 'Merry Christmas. You are making a huge mistake!' or 'Seasons greetings. Why don't you tell James Welsh-Pearson to take a long walk off a short pier?' doesn't seem to be in the spirit of the festive season.

Thursday, 21 December

Last day of school today. We had the best school Christmas party ever. Mr Cluff must have hidden hundreds of candy canes for the treasure hunt. I was one of the losers and I found eight. Miss McKenzie, Nick and Gary taught us all their Scottish Christmas fling to the bagpipes, and Davo and Mr Cluff raced each other on Davo's BMX track. Davo won because Mr Cluff's trousers got caught in the chain and he crashed into a gumtree.

Mrs Whittington brought over a yellow tea cosy for Gabby and four enormous steamed golden syrup puddings for us all to eat.

'Happy Valentine's Day! Happy Valentine's Day!' she said over and over again.

Lucy ran rabbit races where we all got our own bunny with a number painted on its back. Banjo's rabbit was first over the line, but it got disqualified because it kept on running and disappeared into the state forest.

We all gathered around the tank stand for Banjo's end-of-year poetry recital. He had some ripper poems about the circus, crew cuts and squashed salami sandwiches, but the best of all was his poem about giant zucchinis. Sam was moved to tears by it!

Right at the end of the day, Harry Wilson set off in his aeroplane for Greenland. He was wearing all his warmest winter clothes because, even though it was a stinking hot 39°C here at the Bake, he knew it would be well below zero in Greenland.

Harry kissed Miss McKenzie goodbye and wished her a happy Christmas. He shook Mr Cluff's hand and Mr Cluff wished him Godspeed.

He climbed into his plane, put on his orange stack hat, his flying goggles and his mum's yellow rubber gloves and waved goodbye. Ben, Tom, Gary, Jack, Davo and Ned pushed the plane as fast as they could across the playground until the wings fell off and Harry fell through the bottom of the fuselage. Tom and Gary stumbled on over Harry, and Ben fell on top of him.

Harry was pretty disappointed. His bottom lip began to wobble, but he didn't cry. He said he should have stuck with his original plan of travelling to Greenland by hot air balloon. Mr Cluff said not to worry, there was always next year.

The only damper on the day was when Mat turned all mature while we were waiting for the bus. She gave Miss McKenzie a hug and one of those daft air kisses — the ones where you put your cheek about five centimetres away from the other person's cheek, pucker your lips like you've been sucking a lemon and go '*Mwaah!*'

WHAT'S THE POINT???

I was pretty sad to be saying goodbye to Miss McKenzie, but I suppose I'll see her again in six days' time at the engagement party.

Mr Cluff looked kind of sad at all the goodbyes too. Don't know why. You'd think he'd be glad to get rid of Wes and Fez for a while.

Anyway, now I'm home and on holidays. Petal is snuggled up beside me in bed and Sophie is flicking through my bridesmaid book again. She told me she likes the pink raw silk in the style with the shoestring straps and A-line skirt, but for all I understand she could just have said something very rude about the Bolivian President's pet armadillo, Frederico, having bad breath! Wedding, wedding, wedding … yackety, yackety, yack … blah, blah, blah …

Friday, 22 December

Mum took Sophie and me to Dubbo today. We went Christmas shopping and ate out for lunch — a girls' celebration of Mum's birthday. Sophie and I had two iced chocolates each, even though Sophie pretended she was on a diet, and Mum had a glass of champagne.

We were having a great day until Mum said we had to go shopping for dresses for Miss McKenzie's engagement party. I nearly vomited — and believe me, there's a lot that can come up after chicken ricotta rolls, baked potatoes and two iced chocolates.

Sophie was beside herself with excitement and must have tried on 600 dresses that all looked exactly the same before she found the perfect one. I chose the first decent dress I saw — blue with no frills or ribbons or flowers. Mum said it looked lovely on me and insisted on buying a blue headband and white patent leather shoes. Who does she think I am? Matilda Jane the Mature or something? (Patent, by the way, is the mysterious, mature, fashion word for shiny. Go figure!)

Wes and Fez have been trying to learn how to juggle all day. The fruit bowl is full of squashed pears and apples.

Saturday, 23 December

Got up early to do Christmas cooking with Mum and Sophie. We made two dozen fruit mince tarts, a pavlova, a slab of rocky road and a plum pudding the size of an overgrown wombat. Sadly, someone left the back screen door unlatched. Gertrude charged in and ate half the mince tarts and the whole plum pudding. She was as fat as a bloated blue whale.

I don't suppose it really matters. Christmas is going to be a quiet one this year because Dad is racing to finish harvest in time for Miss McKenzie's engagement party. It will just be us for lunch, then over to the Sweeneys' for Christmas drinks in the evening.

Went to the Country Women's Association Christmas party this afternoon. Mat ran up to Sophie squealing and gave her not one, but THREE air kisses. Who does that girl think she is? A French movie star or something?

Even worse, Sophie gave three air kisses back to Mat. Good grief!

MWAH! MWAH! MWAH!

Sophie and Mat went feral talking about Miss McKenzie's wedding, rolling their eyes and fanning their faces. I got dizzy just watching them, so I went outside with Grace and Lynette. We took a whole plate of chocolate crackles up in the melaleuca tree and played Truth or Dare. I dared Grace to go inside and nick a whole chocolate cake for us to eat. She came back with a chocolate cake and a cream sponge.

I got such a tummy ache. When I came home I lay down on my bed and moaned. Petal lay down beside me and whined. She's such a copy cat.

Sunday, 24 December

Sophie and I spent the morning delivering sandwiches and tea to Mum, Dad and Peter out on the trucks and the harvester. Couldn't take them any apples. They're all bruised and rotting in the chook bucket.

Things sure are looking great with the harvest. Good crops are like gold!

After lunch Mum asked us to wrap the Christmas presents. Sophie wrapped mine and I wrapped hers so we didn't find out what we were getting. Mum must be exhausted from being so busy throughout harvesting, because she has bought Wes and Fez a book called *Chemistry at Home*. Dangerous! I stuck it right at the back of the presents, halfway in behind the dresser, so hopefully they won't find it.

Wes, Fez, Sophie and I had our own Christmas Eve tea. Mum, Dad and Peter decided they'd work all night long to finish harvesting the final paddocks.

We spread a picnic out under the peppercorn tree, with chicken sandwiches, lemonade, mince tarts, a pavlova with strawberries and cream and rocky road. Sophie and I had made sandwiches for the pigs out of stale bread and peanut butter, but they decided they liked our food better. By the time we'd dragged them away, there was lemonade and a bit of rocky road for our tea.

Wes and Fez are tucked up in bed now, thank goodness. Sophie and I told them Santa wouldn't come if they weren't asleep by nine o'clock.

Sophie is braiding my hair as I write this and then I have promised to braid hers. I hope she has an instruction book!

Monday, 25 December, Christmas Day
Merry Christmas!

Goodwill to all men ... but not to naughty boys like Wes and Fez.

Mum, Dad and Peter got in at 4 am and slept until 11 am. In the meantime, Wes and Fez opened their presents (and most of Dad's and

Peter's!) and exploded white muck all over their bedroom walls and ceiling. Who knew bicarb soda and vinegar could be so explosive when mixed together and sealed in snap-lock bags? That chemistry book was a *huge* mistake!

Sophie and I cooked bacon and eggs for everyone's brunch and Mum and Dad fell asleep for the rest of the day. I suppose it's been a long, tiring harvest.

Sophie, Peter, Wes, Fez and I tried to play this quiz game Mum and Dad gave me called 'Brains Galore', but it sort of fell flat. Wes, Fez and Peter haven't got enough brains between the three of them to fill a peanut shell, let alone provide any *real* competition in a game where you have to have lots of brains. So it was a pretty quiet day, except for when Mildred and Doris got into a fight over a chocolate bickie while we were coaxing them onto the truck to take them to the Sweeneys'.

Had the best night ever out at the Sweeneys'. Everyone's finished harvesting, and it's been a bumper wheat crop at last after all those tough years of drought. The grown-ups were pretty relaxed and happy.

All the kids had this crazy five-a-side tennis competition. Every time we messed up a shot, we had to put on an extra piece of clothing. Mat was so busy staring at Gavin O'Donnell, trying to get him to notice her, that she kept missing the ball. Five minutes into the game she was wearing so many clothes that she could barely move. She fell over running for the ball and couldn't get up again. She just rolled around helplessly with her arms and legs sticking out like a turtle that's been flipped onto its back. Gavin noticed her *then*, but I don't think it was the kind of attention she was looking for.

Mr Sweeney brought out his banjo after dark and suggested a bush dance, so Dad grabbed his violin, Mrs Hartley borrowed a guitar and Mrs Sweeney got the men to shove her old piano out onto the back veranda. It was great fun. Everyone danced until they dropped. Except for Mat's pop. He danced until his *pants* dropped. Sophie got over-enthusiastic during Strip the Willow and accidentally snapped his braces while she was spinning him around. Mat's pop ended up with his pants around his ankles, yelling,

'It's Strip the *Willow*, not Strip the *Old Man*!'

We nearly died laughing … except for Matilda Jane the Mature who nearly died of embarrassment.

Anyway, it ended all right for Mat, because now Gavin reckons the Sweeneys are a crack-up, and he danced the last three songs with her. I think he was hoping she would do something really stupid, but Mat thought it was because he wants to marry her. I've never seen anyone flutter their eyelashes and roll their eyes so much. I really don't know how she kept her balance throughout the Virginia Reel.

Just when everyone thought the excitement was over for the night, Wes and Fez appeared from down the driveway, wearing tea cosies on their heads and riding their pig chariots. They

got us all to sit in a big circle and ran the chariots round and round inside. Once the pigs were in a routine, Fez stood up in his chariot and started juggling apples, pears and bananas and, I have to say, it was *spectacular*.

Wes then stood up in his chariot, lit a candle and balanced it in a special stand on top of his tea cosy. That's when Mum excused herself and went inside for a little lie-down on Mrs Sweeney's sofa.

Wes and Doris trotted round and round the circus ring with a candle flickering above them. Fez and Mildred trotted round and round with fruit juggling above them. It looked incredible and they should have quit while they were ahead. But it always has to get bigger and better with the Flying Ferals.

Just when we thought the act was complete, Wes started to climb out of his chariot and onto Doris's back! I think he was planning to do the standing gallop, just like the clowns at the circus did on the ponies.

As Wes started to crawl onto Doris, he tipped his head forward and hot wax dripped from the candle onto Doris's back. Doris let out a hideous squeal and reared up on her hind legs. Wes was thrown to the ground where Mildred and Fez ran over the top of him, tearing his tea cosy, bruising his ear and breaking two of his fingers. Fez was thrown from his chariot and tumbled along the grass until he collided with Mr Hartley's knee. Three apples and a banana came down on Gavin's head and knocked him sideways into Mat. Mat took it as another sign of affection and was on an emotional high for the rest of the night. Doris and Mildred charged out across Mrs Sweeney's garden, pulling out seven geraniums and two rose bushes. Lynette laughed so much she peed her pants.

Sensational!

Happy Christmas!

Peace on earth ... but never around Wes and Fez.

Tuesday, 26 December — In the car

We've been driving all day long — Mum, Sophie, Wes, Fez and I — heading towards Bundanoon, Hathaway Homestead and the ENGAGEMENT PARTY. Dad and Peter are in the ute, because they had to deliver a ram to someone at Yeoval on the way.

Petal is looking a bit carsick, so I'm pointing her towards Fez, just in case ...

We're staying in a cottage on the Welsh-Pearson property. Hope it doesn't have as many cobwebs and mice as our shearers' cottage at home.

Maybe this time we'll get to meet James Welsh-Pearson properly. All we saw of him last time was a big bunch of roses, a pale white face and a lot of blood.

10 pm — Hathaway Homestead Guest Palace

James Welsh-Pearson talks with a plum in his mouth and walks like he's got a cricket bat shoved up his bum. I thought he walked that way at Hillrose Poo because Gunther had mauled his leg, but he *always* walks like that.

His mother is even worse. Mrs Welsh-Pearson talks with a *watermelon* in her mouth and smiles without showing her teeth. She calls Sophie Sophia, calls me Trudy, and calls Wes and Fez Wesley and Finlay. She looks down her nose at Wes and Fez as though they're wild animals.

Actually, they *are* wild animals, but *I'm* allowed to say that because I'm family. You're meant to be polite to guests, even when it's Wes and Fez. *Even* if they are wearing tea cosies on their heads.

The Welsh-Pearsons have a house on the harbour in Sydney, but Hathaway Homestead is their hobby farm where they hang out at weekends and on holidays. The grass is green and the fences are all painted white. The barns and sheds look a thousand times fancier than our mud and guts house back home at Hillrose Poo. They have sheep that wear *coats* to keep their wool clean and soft, stud alpacas whose fleece gets sold to textile artists in Europe (huh???!!!!) and a beautiful jersey cow called Jacinta who has won Academy Awards for producing the creamiest milk in the universe (or something like that).

The jersey cow has been quite a problem for Dad. Mrs Welsh-Pearson's name is Clarissa, but Dad keeps calling her Jacinta by mistake. She is not amused.

Dinner at Hathaway Homestead was agony. There were about ten pieces of cutlery for each of us, and Mum kept making these big, dramatic movements every time a new course was served, to demonstrate which knife or fork or spoon we should be using. I still ended up with three knives for eating my dessert. Dad spilt red wine on the tablecloth and kept saying, 'I'm truly sorry, Jacinta.'

And I don't think Mrs Welsh-Pearson was very happy about Petal standing at the back door quacking hysterically to be let in. I tried to explain imprinting and separation anxiety, but she wasn't interested. She really just wanted to tell us all about her late husband and how much she and James miss him.

When dessert came, Fez said, 'Mr Welsh-Pearson really is incredibly late. If he doesn't come soon, dinner will be completely over!'

Miss McKenzie burst out laughing, but soon stopped when she realised James and Mrs Welsh-Pearson were frowning.

The only good thing all evening was when Miss McKenzie and James asked Sophie if she'd like to be the fourth bridesmaid at their wedding. Sophie was overwhelmed with joy. She giggled and fanned her face with her serviette and hugged Miss McKenzie and James. She air kissed Mrs Welsh-Pearson on each cheek with a loud *Mwah!* and Mrs WP seemed delighted! At least *one* of us has made a good impression.

The cottage, by the way, is nothing like our shearers' cottage. It is two storeys and has three bedrooms, two bathrooms and a big box of chocolates on the coffee table.

Well, it *did* have a big box of chocolates on the coffee table ... until Sophie and I discovered it!

Wednesday, 27 December — Day of the engagement party

I must be happy for Miss McKenzie's sake.

I must be happy for Miss McKenzie's sake.

I must be happy for Miss McKenzie's sake.

I must be happy for Miss McKenzie's sake.

I must be happy for Miss McKenzie's sake.

I must be happy for Miss McKenzie's sake.

Well, that's the engagement party over.

Wes and Fez disappeared soon after breakfast. They'd discovered an alpaca that liked to spit, so they spent the whole day running back and forth across the paddock, dodging slimy green goop.

Mr Cluff arrived at 12.30 looking like a bloodhound who was just fed a bowl of carrot sticks. The only time he looked happy was when Miss McKenzie was talking to him.

The Sweeneys arrived at one, and Mat burst out of the car throwing air kisses everywhere.

She positively *swooned* when Sophie told her that she was also going to be a bridesmaid.

Mrs WP thinks Mat and Lynette are little angels, so now I'm the only one in her bad books. Anyone would think I'd fallen over and got grass stains down the front of my new blue dress on purpose.

I have to admit, the party was lovely. There were five long tables on the front lawn, covered in white cloths and big bunches of pink roses. There was a live band — much calmer than the stuff Dad, Mr Sweeney and Mrs Hartley play, but it was beautiful, just the same. We stood and ate loads of tiny sandwiches and pastries. Then just when we thought we'd burst, they sat us down for lunch!

Mat, Sophie, Lynette and I sat with James's cousins from Sydney. Sophie was beside herself because it turns out she goes to boarding school in Bathurst with James's cousin's boyfriend's sister's best friend's piano teacher's daughter — or something like that.

During the speeches James's friend Alex said some very nice things about James that *might* have been true, but I haven't noticed anything so great about him yet. Then Dad gave a speech as Miss McKenzie's pretend father for the day. He said some very sweet things about Miss McKenzie that were all totally true. Then he said that we are like family at Hardbake Plains, and it's traditional for the bride's family to provide the wedding. So, he would like to formally invite everyone to join James and Katherine at HILLROSE POO for the occasion of their wedding!!!

Everyone from Hardbake Plains cheered, but the Sydney friends and family looked stunned, disappointed, or both. Mrs WP and James looked like they had just sucked on some extra-sour lemons.

An awkward hush fell over the party.

Dad started to look embarrassed. It was obvious that Hillrose Poo wasn't good enough.

But Miss McKenzie, with her sparkly eyes and heart of gold, stepped forward to save the day. She threw her arms around Dad, gave him a sloppy kiss on the cheek and cried, 'Och! That would be just grand, Robert!'

She gave James one of her dazzling, freckly smiles where her whole face shines, so of course he agreed.

A wedding at Hillrose Poo!

I suppose this means she really is going to marry this bloke.

Thursday, 28 December —
Hathaway Homestead ... Still!

Mum is a traitor!

And on Sophie's birthday too!

Petal and I woke Sophie this morning with a mug of tea and fifteen chocolate frogs — one for each year. I gave her a novel called *Love on the Seas*, which, from the cover, looks like a story about a lovesick pirate and a lady who wears far too much lipstick. It nearly killed me to buy it, but I knew Sophie would think it was drop-dead romantic, and it only cost three dollars. Petal gave Sophie a duckling kiss and pooped on her pillow.

Mum and Dad gave Sophie clothes and jewellery, Peter gave her a CD by a band called Festering Punks, and Wes and Fez gave her a huge, brown, spotty slug they'd found outside their bedroom window last night. Things were going just fine.

Until Mum announced that Mat, Lynette, Sophie and I are all staying here with Miss McKenzie, James and Mrs WP for a week (HELP!!!), while *they* get to go home to Hillrose Poo.

Mrs WP wants to make sure we get our bridesmaids dresses sorted out while we're here.

I *thought* my suitcase looked too big for just three days away.

Mum didn't tell me earlier because she knew I'd kick up a fuss.

Worse still, Mum took Petal with her. Petal looked devastated as they drove off. I hope she doesn't pine away and die while we're apart.

Wes and Fez went home as happy as two kookaburras at a worm farm because James gave them the spitting alpaca. Dad and Peter took it on the ute. James said he wanted to get rid of it because it kept spitting on visitors. Wes and Fez said they'd *love* it because it would spit on visitors. Mum said no, but Dad pointed out that alpacas are good for keeping wild dogs away from your sheep. *I'm* hoping it'll be good for keeping wild brothers away from the house.

Anyway, it was kind of James to give the spitting beast to Wes and Fez. Maybe he's not so bad after all.

Lynette, Mat and Sophie are getting on like a house on fire with Mrs WP. They are acting like princesses, fluttering their eyelashes and air kissing. They hold their little fingers out to the side when they drink cups of tea and eat microscopic slices of Sophie's tasteless, white birthday cake. Mat is starting to talk with a plum in her mouth.

I'm pretending to have a tummy ache so I can hide out at the cottage for the rest of the day. I seem to have more in common with Sophie's birthday slug than with anyone else around here.

I miss Petal.

Friday, 29 December

Sophie showed Miss McKenzie and Mrs WP her bridesmaid dress design this morning and they both thought it was beautiful. Sophie was so proud.

We spent the day in Bowral at Mrs WP's dressmaker and must have tried on at least twenty different dresses. Every time Mat, Sophie or Lynette came out of the dressing room, Mrs WP would smile and say they looked just gorgeous. But every time I came out of the dressing room she frowned. She would straighten seams and hemlines, and sigh like she was truly suffering.

Once, when she looked particularly depressed at my appearance and started to massage her throbbing temples, I offered to give up my role as bridesmaid. Honestly, it was the first time Mrs WP seemed pleased with me. She beamed, and called me darling.

But Miss McKenzie stepped in and said, 'Och no! What are you saying, Blue? You will be the most beautiful bridesmaid ever, with your red hair and sweet freckles. I'll be devastated if you aren't one of my special girls.'

So there you go. I was bound to disappoint one of them. Mrs WP would be devastated if I *was* a bridesmaid. Miss McKenzie would be devastated if I *wasn't*. I think that's what you call a lose–lose situation.

Of course, my loyalties lie with Miss McKenzie, so I'm still going to wear a pink dress and limp up the aisle like I've got a chunk of shrapnel in my leg, with Mrs WP frowning and sighing at me all the way.

Saturday, 30 December

All day at the dressmaker's again.

BORING.

Mat, Sophie and Lynette don't seem to mind. Maybe it's because they're not as intelligent as me. Simple-minded folk are easily amused. Just look at Wes and Fez.

Used the wrong fork for dessert tonight. You'd think I'd stolen the last scrap of bread from a starving orphan by the way Mrs WP glared at me.

Miss McKenzie had gone out for dinner with James, so I didn't even have her to smile encouragingly at me.

Went back to the cottage early with a *real* tummy ache.

Sunday, 31 December

This has been the most boring New Year's Eve ever.

Miss McKenzie and James have gone up to Sydney for a party so we've been stuck here with Mrs WP and six of her friends, learning to play mah jong. I reckon mah jong could be really cool, but not when you have to sit in your best dress (the grass stains came out nicely, so I don't know what all the fuss was about), eating prawns on miniature pieces of toast and drinking weak tea with no milk or sugar, while your little finger sticks out at an awkward angle.

Thank goodness Mrs Parnell brought along her miniature sausage dog, Strudel, otherwise the whole evening would have been a complete waste of time. After I'd spilt my second cup of tea, I hid under the table with Strudel and taught him how to beg using little bits of raw steak I found in the fridge. He was doing really well, until I accidentally tossed one of the pieces of meat into Mrs Falkner-Smythe's handbag. Strudel went berserk trying to find it. He ended up mauling her lace hanky, her purse, a photo of her grandchildren and the arm of her sunglasses before he found the steak. Then he chewed the bow off Mrs WP's cream patent leather shoes!

I pretended to have another stomach ache and went back to the cottage before anyone discovered the damage. Sophie came over soon after and is sitting with me now. She's bored too, despite all the fabric and air kissing. I told her about Strudel and she laughed until she cried.

If we were home, we'd be running around playing spotlight while Dad and Bert Hartley dislocated each other's shoulders in arm wrestles. Mum would serve up mountains of cakes and sausage rolls and jugs of fizzy drink, and Mr Sweeney would play his banjo. Nobody would get into trouble for using the wrong spoon for their custard or getting grass stains on their clothes.

I'm homesick.

January

Monday, 1 January —
New Year's Day

Happy New Year!

Miss McKenzie and James took us bushwalking down in Morton National Park today. It's beautiful — damp and green with giant tree ferns. We saw a real waterfall that flows all year round. Imagine having so much water. Petal would have loved it.

We hired three tandem bikes in Bundanoon. It was heaps of fun. Mat and I were totally out of control. Mat just doesn't get that you can't steer from the back seat. We ran into Miss McKenzie and James and knocked them into a blackberry bush. Miss McKenzie ripped the back of her shorts so you could see that she was wearing pink and orange striped knickers. It was hilarious. She couldn't stand up straight for ten minutes, she laughed so much.

James, however, didn't think it was very funny at all. He blushed like a tomato and made her wrap his jumper around her waist. We had to go straight back to Hathaway Homestead, even though we'd been planning to buy ice creams from the café.

Mrs WP was horrified when we told her at dinner time what had happened. She acted all sympathetic towards Miss McKenzie and said, 'You poor dear.' But Miss McKenzie got helpless with laughter all over again and snorted chocolate mousse out her nose.

Wasn't Mrs WP upset at that!

James didn't look too pleased either.

I don't get what the problem was. It really was funny. Even Mat couldn't help laughing.

If looks could kill, we'd all be dead now from Mrs WP's glare.

HEE! HEE! HEE! HEE! HEE!

Tuesday, 2 January

All day at the dressmaker's again.

I think even Mat is getting fed up with it all.

She must have been so bored, because she forgot herself and burped out loud.

I think Mrs WP will be glad to have Hathaway Homestead to herself again.

One more day to go!

Wednesday, 3 January

Miss McKenzie brought her bagpipes down to the cottage today so we could practise the bridal waltz. Nobody told me we had to dance at this wedding!

I think my shrapnel wound flares up even more for waltzing than it does for the bridesmaid's walk. It didn't bother Miss McKenzie, though. She laughed until she got the hiccups, and made me promise to dance exactly the same way at her wedding.

That's what's so great about Miss McKenzie. She likes people just as they are.

We were having a lovely time. Sophie and Lynette were dancing together, Mat was dancing with a cushion, pretending it was Gavin O'Donnell, and I was limping around like an uncoordinated camel, when Mrs WP came down to the cottage looking very concerned.

I thought, here we go again. It's time to be disappointed in Blue.

But it wasn't *me* she was disappointed with. It was Miss McKenzie!

Apparently, the bagpipes are not really the RIGHT KIND of instrument to play in Welsh-Pearson circles. Mrs WP talked about her friend Dorothea Armstrong-Brett, whose daughter-in-law plays the flute in the Sydney Symphony Orchestra … and Julia Cameron, a friend of a friend, who plays Baroque music on the crumhorn, and how simply enchanting it all was.

What does *a friend of a friend* mean?

And what on earth is a *crumhorn*??? Sounds seriously painful — like something Mr Sweeney's bull might get if it ran full-speed into a red gum gate post.

When Mrs WP left, I noticed James standing behind the hedge. I think Miss McKenzie did too because she looked very sad all of a sudden.

I'm glad we're going home tomorrow. I just wish Miss McKenzie was coming with us.

Thursday, 4 January —
Hillrose Poo, at last!

Bliss!

I'm home, sitting on the veranda, eating lamingtons. Petal is in my lap. Fluffles is rubbing against my leg. Gertrude is drooling at my feet. The hot, dry wind is blowing in my face.

Bliss!

Miss McKenzie drove us home to Hillrose Poo, even though she was only meant to take us to Bathurst, where Mrs Sweeney was going to meet us and take us the rest of the way.

Miss McKenzie told James and Mrs WP that she had *changed her mind* about staying at Hathaway Homestead for the holidays, and that she wanted to drive us *all the way home*. She also seemed to think it was very important that they noticed her putting her *bagpipes* in the boot of the car, and that they realised that she *liked to play the bagpipes every single day of her life*.

When we said goodbye, Miss McKenzie gave James an AIR KISS.

Miss McKenzie is *not* an air kisser!

Wes and Fez must have missed us. They met us at the front gate to Hillrose Poo and insisted on driving Sophie and me home in the pig chariots.

Wes and Sophie crashed, and Sophie grazed half the skin off her nose.

Gunther greeted me by getting his ducklings to attack the minute I stepped out of Fez's pig chariot. Petal greeted me by collapsing on my feet and sighing with joy. She hasn't left my side since.

Miss McKenzie is staying the night in the sleep-out. She lives in town with Mrs Whittington at Magpie's Rest, but Mrs Whittington is away, visiting her niece in Dubbo. Miss McKenzie couldn't bear the thought of being on her own tonight. Besides, Hillrose Poo is such a great place to stay.

There's no place like home!

Friday, 5 January

Wes and Fez spent half the morning teasing Macka the alpaca, trying to make him spit. Sophie, Peter and I sat on the back veranda eating watermelon, laughing ourselves stupid.

'Buck-toothed barnacle!' cried Wes.

'Knock-kneed numbskull!' yelled Fez.

'Pea-brained puffball!' snarled Wes.

'Leech-livered lily-pants!' hissed Fez.

Macka just stood there, blinking.

'If brains were dynamite you wouldn't have enough to blow your nose.'

'You're so dumb, when you got locked in the supermarket you nearly starved to death!'

'You're so boring, I've had better conversations with a teapot.'

'You're as ugly as a bucket full of pig snouts.'

Fez ran around and around, leaping up and down. Wes stuck his bottom out and made a rude noise.

Macka just stared out across the paddocks. He refused to spit.

Wes and Fez were disgusted. They stormed off to race their pig chariots.

After they left, Peter spat a watermelon seed on the grass. Macka walked over to Peter and spat in his face.

Miss McKenzie is staying again tonight. She spent most of the day drinking cups of tea and eating lamingtons with Mum.

Hope she leaves some for Sophie and me.

Saturday, 6 January

Miss McKenzie cried and ate chocolate biscuits all day. She didn't even share any with Gertrude. Gerty really loves chocolate biscuits, and Miss McKenzie usually loves Gerty.

I tried to cheer her up by pointing out that the scab on Sophie's nose looks like New Zealand. There's even a North Island and South Island. She didn't crack a smile.

Wes and Fez rode past in their pig chariots, wearing tea cosies on their heads, juggling apples and bananas. That *did* bring a smile to her face for a while. Especially when Doris galloped under the clothesline and Wes got tangled up in the sheets. But then she went back to sniffling and weeping.

By the time she left we'd run out of tissues.

I just don't know what we can do. Miss McKenzie doesn't normally let anything get her down. It's awful to see.

I asked Mum what I could do to help. She said Miss McKenzie just needs some space.

'Time heals all, Blue,' Mum said.

I pointed out that it hadn't healed Wes and Fez of their stupidity, but she didn't think that was the same thing.

Sophie said that love isn't always as easy as people hope, and started talking about *Love on the Seas*, the book I gave her for her birthday.

Good grief!

What is it with everyone and love these days? All I need now is for Matilda Jane the Mature to visit and tell me all about her plans to marry Gavin O'Donnell and spend her evenings going to the opera and balls …

Sunday, 7 January

Sophie and I were feeding the chooks this morning when Macka appeared from nowhere and spat at Sophie through the wire. Sophie screamed. Macka threw his head back and gurgled with joy.

Wes and Fez were devastated when we told them.

'Why won't Macka spit at me?' said Fez, and burst out crying.

Mat rang tonight to tell me that she is getting a horse. Her dad is bringing

79

it home tomorrow and she wants Sophie and me to come over and see it. I can't wait. I love horses.

Monday, 8 January

Sheba is beautiful. She is enormous and white and the gentlest horse you could ever find. We spent the morning climbing all over her, brushing her tail and mane. Mat even let me, Lynette and Sophie ride her around the stockyard.

Mr Sweeney got Sheba for free. Her owners were going to put her down. Why would they want to destroy such a beautiful creature?

Mat is so lucky.

When we got home, Wes and Fez were heading out the back to *bribe* Macka into spitting.

'My pocket's full of choc bits,' said Wes.

'We'll give one to Macka every time he spits,' said Fez.

It might have worked, except Doris and Mildred's bionic hearing alerted them to the sound of choc bits rattling together. They bolted around the corner of the house and knocked Wes to the ground just as he stepped off the veranda. They snuffled at his pocket until his shorts were torn and all the choc bits were vacuumed into their enormous piggy stomachs.

Macka the alpaca appeared from nowhere and ran around Wes, gurgling in delight.

Tuesday, 9 January

Macka spat at Mum through the kitchen window while she was washing the breakfast dishes this morning. Wes and Fez bolted outside and ran around Macka, jumping and shouting.

They didn't seem to bother Macka one bit, but they annoyed the guts out of Gunther. He squealed, leapt off the veranda, knocked Fez over and pinned him to the ground. His ducklings charged and pecked at Fez's nose and ears. Fez shook his head from side to side, yelling in agony.

Macka lay down in the shade and gurgled happily.

Wednesday, 10 January

Miss McKenzie is a basket case and, I have to say, it's not very attractive. I thought being in love was meant to make people happy and beautiful.

She spent all evening at the Sweeneys' barbecue with Mum, Mrs Sweeney and Mrs O'Donnell, crying and snotting in a most unladylike fashion — which just proves that she and James are not suited to each other.

Mrs WP would be *mortified* if she could hear the way Miss McKenzie blew her nose like a trumpet. She'd probably talk about Serena Squid-Harpoon, a friend of a friend, who sounded like a piccolo flute when she blew her nose, or Babette Intestinal-Abscess, her dearest niece, who didn't even produce snot, but just gave ladylike dabs at the corner of her nostrils with her handkerchief when she was emotional.

For once I actually *wanted* to talk with Mat about THE WEDDING, because I'm more confused than ever. But Mat was too busy trying to get Gavin's attention. She fluttered her eyelashes and smoothed her hair behind her ears until I thought it would fall out. Then, at supper time, she made a grand entrance on Sheba. Sadly for Mat, an unbelievably bad smell made a grand entrance at the same time.

'Pooh! Mat!' shouted Wes. 'What did you eat for dinner?'

'Amazing!' cried Peter. 'You should bottle that and sell it to the army as a weapon of mass destruction!'

'Don't anyone light a match!' yelled Gavin, laughing.

Mat's face crumpled up in a blotchy lump. She slipped off Sheba and ran inside, crying.

Poor Mat.

Mr Sweeney ran over and led Sheba away before she could share any more wind. When he came back, I asked him if that was why her owners were going to put her down.

Mr Sweeney nodded and said, 'Poor horse. Bit of gas never hurt anyone.'

I think Mat would beg to differ ...

Thursday, 11 January

Mat phoned this morning, bawling her eyes out. 'Gavin thinks that smell was me. He thinks I stink!' she sobbed.

I didn't know what to say. I know less about L-O-V-E than anyone else I know (except Wes and Fez, of course, and they don't count).

Mum and Dad have loved each other for twenty years, so they're obviously experts.

Peter was once in love — with Chantelle O'Brien in year four. He used to give her a patty cake every recess, until he realised she was also accepting Anzac biscuits from Trevor Parker every lunch time. Peter felt totally betrayed and was heartbroken for at least three days (which just goes to show that love can make a big mess of everything!).

Sophie is in love with every punk rocker she has ever listened to, and is an expert on love after reading hundreds of novels with names like *Love in the Mountains* or *Stolen Kisses*.

Matilda Jane the Mature actually kissed a boy on the jetty last summer when she was at the beach and is, of course, an expert on having her heart crushed time and time again by the one and only Gavin O'Donnell. Tragically, Gavin O'Donnell doesn't even know what a heartless boyfriend he is because he doesn't even know that he is *anyone's* boyfriend, let alone Mat's!!! Yet she still doesn't know what to do when love gets tangled up with foul odours!

Even silly Nick Farrel is in love with Lynette Sweeney and protects her like a faithful guard dog.

Me?

I'm just confused.

Friday, 12 January

Macka, Gunther and the ducklings have formed one happy family. They sleep together in the long grass under the peppercorn tree.

Wes and Fez are disgusted.

'What's the use of an alpaca that doesn't spit on us?' said Wes.

'It's like a poo without flies,' said Fez.

'Or a dam without leeches,' said Wes.

'Or a circus without acrobats,' said Peter.

Good on you, Peter. Now the Flying Ferals have forgotten Macka and are back into the circus stunts. Last thing I heard, they were talking about catapults …

Saturday, 13 January

Wes, Fez and Peter made a little seesaw today — the Flying Ferals Catapult Prototype #1. They set it up in Wes and Fez's bedroom, facing towards Wes's bed, and sat Fez's big, blue teddy on it. Fez explained that the real catapult, when they build it, will be a big one. They'll set it up outside and fling Wes towards the trampoline, so he will be completely safe.

Sure!

Fez stood on a chair and jumped down onto the opposite end of the seesaw to Teddy. Teddy flew upwards into the rapidly spinning blades of the ceiling fan. His head flew straight out the window and his body plopped to the floor.

Sophie screamed. Petal ran around in circles, quacking and flapping her wings. Tufts of blue fur and white stuffing drifted onto the beds.

Fez lay on the floor, hugging Teddy's headless body and crying his guts out, 'Teddy's dead! Teddy's dead!'

Wes and Peter staggered around laughing.

I grabbed Petal, and snuck out to feed the chooks so that I was well out of sight by the time Mum came in and let rip.

Sunday, 14 January

It's officially over.

Miss McKenzie came out after Mass to tell Mum and Dad that the engagement is off.

Surprisingly, she didn't cry a single tear or eat a single lamington to keep her spirits up.

I tried to look concerned, but I couldn't wipe the smile off my face. I was right and everyone else was wrong. This wedding was a huge mistake. Marrying James Welsh-Pearson would have been a disaster.

Miss McKenzie belongs at Hardbake Plains. She's only been here for a year but she is part of this place and it is part of her.

Before she left this afternoon, I said, 'You've got red dirt between your toes.'

She looked down at her sandals and laughed.

Monday, 15 January

Sophie, Mat and Lynette are distraught because they can no longer be bridesmaids.

Sophie sat on the veranda all afternoon, listening to her Festering Punks CD, clutching my bridesmaid's scrapbook to her chest. Every now and then she'd sigh.

Gerty lay on the veranda, listening to the Festering Punks CD, wagging her tail and rolling her eyes in delight! She was humming along in her fat piggy head, just like she does with the bagpipes. Weird.

Mat rang and blubbered on about what a terrible mistake Miss McKenzie was making. How could she possibly break off an engagement to such a wonderful man as James Welsh-Pearson who had so much money and was a lawyer and lived in Sydney, and Mrs Welsh-Pearson was so kind and generous and had such interesting friends and blah, blah, blah, blabber, blabber, blabber.

I told Mat that *she* should marry James Welsh-Pearson if she thought he was so spectacular. Maybe she had a chance with him because, unlike Gavin, he didn't think she had a problem with emitting toxic gases.

Mat burst out crying and said some things that were incredibly immature for someone who tries to be so grown up all the time. And then she hung up!

Why do people get so upset about all this love stuff?

I JUST DON'T GET IT.

Tuesday, 16 January

Had a night out at Hardbake Plains Pub tonight. The grown-ups met to organise the Australia Day picnic race. All of us kids went along and played billiards and darts.

Miss McKenzie was there and she didn't look at all miserable. Why was she so upset when she was engaged to James, but now looks as happy as a pig in a pie shop? It's almost like she's relieved!

But what would I know?

Love is just confusing.

Mr Cluff spent the whole evening beside Miss McKenzie, smiling and laughing. He was obviously trying to take her mind off things. He's the kindest man.

Mat is still mega-embarrassed about the Sheba gas incident and is avoiding Gavin O'Donnell. It's a shame, because Gavin thinks Mat is great fun. He spent the whole night looking for her.

Mat spent the whole night slinking behind vending machines and ducking into the Ladies. I told her that she was in and out of the toilets so much that now Gavin probably thinks she has diarrhoea as well as wind. I said I know it's painful for her to hear these things, but if she's going to behave in such an immature fashion, someone has to point it out to her. She gave me one of her withering stares.

Sophie and I beat everyone at darts.

Wes beat Lynette at billiards, so Nick hit Wes over the head with a billiard stick. Fez hit Nick over the head with the darts board.

Sunshine, the grumpiest pub owner in Australia, kicked them all out and said they were banned for life.

Wednesday, 17 January

Wes and Fez made the Flying Ferals Life-Sized Catapult today. They set it up in the back yard and aimed it at the trampoline. Petal ran away quacking and flapping her wings before they'd even tried it out.

Wes stood on one end of the catapult, while Fez leapt from the chook shed onto the opposite end. The plank of wood snapped, flew up and smacked Fez in the nose. He fell flat on his back in the stinging nettles.

Macka the alpaca appeared from nowhere and stood over Fez making a joyful gurgling noise.

Mum thinks Fez's nose is broken. She sent him to bed with an icepack and told him not to come out again.

Does she mean *ever*???

Thursday, 18 January

Sophie played her Festering Punks CD again today. Gertrude lay on the veranda beneath our bedroom window, wagging her tail and grunting along to the music for over two hours.

When we played the bagpipes CD tonight, Gerty went psycho. She paced back and forth along the veranda, frothing at the mouth and squealing.

I went out to calm her down but she head-butted me through the fly-screen door, back into the kitchen.

Sophie changed the music to the Festering Punks CD and Gerty settled!!! She stood still and rolled her eyes in delight — just like Mat does when anyone talks about weddings. Finally she lay down for 'Ugly, Ugly, Ugly World', bumping her head against the veranda post every time the line, 'Ugly, ugly, ugly!' was shouted out across the plains.

Mum looked out the window at Gertrude and sighed. She wandered off to her bedroom with a cup of tea, mumbling her own thoughts on what was ugly, ugly, ugly.

A punk rocker pig!

What a crack-up!

Friday, 19 January

'Welcome to My Rubbish Bin' by Festering Punks blasted across the plains at 7.10 am. Mum is not impressed, but Dad said it's better than the bagpipes by a long shot.

Wes and Fez broke Peter's nose today. Something to do with the Flying Ferals catapult and Peter riding past on the motorbike at the wrong time. Dad said Wes and Fez would have to help with the fencing for a few days until Peter is able to work again.

James Welsh-Pearson rang this evening! Thankfully *I* answered the phone and realised who it was before I identified myself. I put on my best Italian accent and said, 'Scusi mamma mia. The spaghetti's boiling over. I have to go. Arrivederci!'

Mum looked a bit suspicious when I told her it was a wrong number.

I hope he isn't ringing Miss McKenzie to beg her to marry him.

Saturday, 20 January

'Presidents and Puppets' by Festering Punks blasted across the plains at 6.35 am. Dad started to sing along as he was getting dressed!

James Welsh-Pearson rang again today. Sophie answered the phone and talked sweetly for five minutes, asking all about Mrs WP and her latest game of mah jong. I signalled for her to hang up, but she pretended not to understand.

I wrote HANG UP YOU SILLY TWIT!!! on a piece of paper, but she turned her back to me and chatted on.

I'm not proud of what I did next but, really, I had no choice …

I put the bagpipes CD on full blast, opened the back door and stood out of the way. Gerty charged in, squealing with anger, and head-butted the first person she saw. Sophie crashed to the floor and skidded under the dining table. The phone flew into the lounge room. Gerty bolted along the hallway and out the front door. I grabbed the phone and hung up.

When James rang back, I pretended he had called an ice-cream shop in Denmark.

And when Sophie blamed me for the enormous bruise on her bum, I pretended it was an innocent mistake.

Dad came home tonight with a swollen thumb and a split lip. Wes and Fez looked like they'd tried to escape a prisoner-of-war camp by running full-speed through the barbed-wire fencing. Dad said Sophie and I would have to help with the fencing on Monday because things didn't work out so well with the twin tornadoes.

Sunday, 21 January

Watched cricket all day.

Just me, Dad, Peter, Petal and a plate of ham sandwiches.

No dodgy phone calls from James Welsh-Pearson.

No emotional phone calls from Matilda Jane the Mature.

No phone calls from *anyone*, for that matter. I pulled the telephone connection out of its socket before breakfast and Mum didn't notice until 10.30 pm. Hee hee!

Total peace and quiet.

Bliss!

Monday, 22 January

James WP rang *again* this morning. What is wrong with that man?

Thankfully Peter answered the phone, because *I* was out fencing with Dad. When Peter realised who it was, he started singing the Malaysian national anthem (learnt from his friend Xiu), just like I'd asked him to. James hung up.

Mat is coming to stay for a week tomorrow. Mr and Mrs Sweeney have a veterinary conference in Sydney. Lynette's staying with Sarah Love.

Gavin is coming to stay for a few days, too, because he reckons Mat is always good for a laugh. Poor Mat. I hope she's over the whole wind and diarrhoea trauma, otherwise she'll be unbearable to live with.

Tuesday, 23 January

Mat and Mr Sweeney arrived at seven this morning, with Sheba in the horse float. Mr Sweeney said Sheba couldn't be left at home on the farm because she has to be given special digestive tablets every morning and night. She's on a strict diet of fresh grass and oats — no carrots, apples, sugar or any other special treats.

Mat blushed like a beetroot. I was very sensitive and didn't mention gas or bowel bacteria or SBDs.

Sheba seems happy enough here at Hillrose Poo. She's hanging out in the long grass with Macka, Gunther and the ducklings. The Festering Punks' music seemed to upset her digestive system at sunset, but the air has been fresh and clear since. Hopefully it will stay that way!

Sophie, Mat and I have moved our stuff into the sleep-out. You can hardly move with three beds all crammed in, but it's fun.

Wednesday, 24 January

Gavin arrived today. Mat has been hiding behind trees, tank stands and veranda posts all day. I don't get it. If it's really love, shouldn't people be happy? Why can't she just clear the air (pardon the pun) about Sheba's gas problem, and have a laugh about it?

Love really turns people's brains to mush.

Poor Mat!

Thank goodness Miss McKenzie came to her senses!

Sophie, Mat and I went swimming in the dam today. Petal was ecstatic, chugging in and out between us, quacking noisily. We were having a great time, drifting around on the tyre tubes, talking about chocolate, until a dead sheep popped up to the surface and started floating around with us.

Gross!

Thursday, 25 January

The New and Improved Flying Ferals Catapult had its first run today.

Fez leapt off the chook shed roof onto the end of the plank, launching a sack full of chook pellets. The sack flew through the air and landed exactly where it was supposed to, right in the middle of the trampoline. Quite impressive really ... until it bounced back up into the air, hit the peppercorn tree, split open and flung chook pellets all over Gunther and his ducks.

Gunther squealed with anger, and chased Peter up the nearest tree.

The ducks flapped their wings and quacked ferociously, chasing Wes up the clothesline.

Macka appeared from nowhere, spat in Gavin's face, then trotted around gurgling merrily.

Fez burst into tears, crying, 'Why won't Macka spit on me?'

We were all killing ourselves laughing when Mat ran across the yard like a maniac, yelling, 'NOOOOOOOOOOOOOOO!!!'

Sheba was gobbling chook pellets as fast as she could before Gerty, Mildred and Doris vacuumed them all up.

Gavin ran after Mat, laughing. 'It's only chook food!'

Mat started crying and blubbered that Sheba was on a special diet. Gavin laughed and said fat horses were funny as. And Mat cried, 'You don't understand!'

But an hour later when Sheba had started digesting the chook pellets, he sure did. We had to move her three paddocks away just so we could breathe without gagging.

Friday, 26 January — Australia Day

The Hardbake Plains Australia Day picnic race was held for the first time in three years today. The last two years it was cancelled because of the drought. This year the track was soft and grassy.

We started at nine with the bacon and eggs breakfast barbie. Mrs Whittington was there, serving eggs. She wore a big, red satin sash that said 'Miss Wool and Wheat'. She kept on telling everyone how proud she was to have won the competition once again. No-one had the heart to tell her that the Harvest Festival pageant hadn't been run for the last forty years.

Sunshine gave the official welcome, reminding everyone that they would probably be dehydrated and have sunstroke by noon. He's such a gloomy-guts.

The Australia Day picnic race is an open race — you can ride anything that doesn't have a motor, as long as it's not a horse. Bikes are always popular. Davo and Gary Hartley both entered on their BMX bikes. Sammy Ferris, Lucy's grandpa, had an old penny-farthing bike and little James Love was on his tricycle.

Mrs Murphy entered on Mr Murphy. Everyone was splitting their sides laughing because Mr Murphy is skinny as a bean pole and Mrs Murphy is quite round and jolly. Jed Murphy, Ned's cousin, was visiting from the Blue Mountains, and he entered on his hang glider. He'd been at the race track since 5 am assembling a tower so he could fly off at the start.

Sunshine had an antique beer-keg barrow with wooden wheels to push Miss McKenzie around in. Harry Wilson and his little sister, Dora, had a sheep each, with fantastic saddles their mum had made. Harry was wearing his flying goggles and Dora was dressed like a proper jockey in pink and purple silk. There were the usual donkeys, cows, a camel and, of course, Wes and Fez in their pig chariots pulled by Doris and Mildred.

Banjo launched the race with his latest poem, 'Ode to the Australia Day Picnic Race':

Bacon, eggs and sausages,
Aussie pride to share,
Racing sheep and bikes and bulls,
Advance Australia Fair!

The starter gun exploded and they were off.

Jed Murphy leapt from the tower in his hang glider and nose-dived straight into Mrs Love's donkey. The donkey kicked and bucked, tossing Mrs Love into Sunshine's beer-keg barrow. Miss McKenzie and Mrs Love screeched with laughter. Sunshine snarled and cursed, and refused to go on.

Mr Murphy piggy-backed Mrs Murphy just five or six paces and had to put her down. Mrs Murphy didn't want to give up that easily, so she threw Mr Murphy over her shoulder and continued to run around the race track.

Harry and Dora Wilson were doing pretty well on their sheep until Tom Gillies' kelpie slipped its collar and rounded them up into the schoolyard.

Wes and Fez galloped to the front in their pig

chariots, screaming and yelling like maniacs, but enough is never enough with those boys. Just as they looked certain to win, they pulled tea cosies onto their heads, stood up and started juggling oranges and pears. Doris veered across the track and knocked Davo and Gary off their BMX bikes. Mildred turned a full circle and ran back into the camel.

Mrs Murphy chugged up from behind and took the lead, with Mr Murphy bobbing over her shoulder. Everyone started to cheer.

Sammy Ferris caught up on his penny-farthing, but Mrs Murphy swung Mr Murphy around until his head caught Sammy in the guts, knocking him to the ground. The crowd went wild. Mrs Murphy waved and smiled, her face like a big, red tomato, dripping with sweat. She bulldozed on, crossed the finish line and dumped Mr Murphy on the grass. She waved her hands above her head like an Olympic champion.

Everyone said it was the most spectacular win ever.

The whole day would have been perfect, except that as we were leaving, Miss McKenzie apologised for the calls James had been making.

Mum said, 'What calls?' but Sophie and I knew — the calls he had made to Italy, Denmark, Malaysia …

Miss McKenzie sighed and said she hoped she'd done the right thing, cancelling the wedding.

I was about to yell, 'Too right you did!' but Mat and Sophie shoved me into the car. Sophie told me to shut up. Mat threatened to tie me up in Sheba's paddock when we got home if I interfered.

What could I do? There would be no point in saving Miss McKenzie from a fate worse than death if I actually died myself …

Saturday, 27 January

Mat and Sophie kept me awake for hours last night, talking about boys and kissing and romance and LOVE. I wanted to puke even more than when I inhaled Sheba's toxic gas the other day.

They have all these rules about how to behave around boys that sound *really* stupid. The most important are:

1. **The Dumb Rule** — <u>Don't act too smart or boys won't like you.</u> They don't want you to make them look dumb. (That one

shouldn't be too difficult for either Sophie or Mat!)

2. **The Food Rule** — <u>*Never* eat in front of boys, because it's not cool.</u> I asked if the boys are allowed to eat in front of the girls. Sophie and Mat both said, 'Duh. Of course they can!' I just don't get it. Why can boys eat, but girls can't?

3. **The Length Rule** — <u>Girls are supposed to have long fingernails, long hair and long eyelashes.</u> I asked if long feet were good, feeling like there might be hope for me some day, if my brain ever turned to mush and I decided I actually *wanted* to fall in love. But they both scoffed and said that big feet were a DISASTER. Boys like dainty little feet.

So, as far as I can see, your feet, appetite and brain have to be tiny. You have to pretend to be someone you are *not*, so that a boy likes you, but the you he ends up liking will be so different from the *real* you, that he doesn't actually like the real you at all!

Phew! Doesn't sound like it's worth the effort to me!

No wonder Miss McKenzie was so miserable when she was engaged to James Welsh-Pearson.

Anyway, Mat obviously thinks it *is* worth the effort …

Sophie, Mat and I were down at the dam today. We were lying on our towels, nibbling on chocolate, when Peter and Gavin rode down on the motorbike. Mat didn't want to be seen eating, because that would be so TOTALLY UNCOOL, but she didn't want to throw her whole block of chocolate in the dam either. I could see a real struggle going on in her attractively tiny brain. Just as the boys arrived, she decided to stuff the whole block in her mouth at once, to conceal the evidence.

Mat's cheeks were bulging. Gavin asked how she was going and she couldn't say a word. She just nodded stupidly and tried to keep the melting chocolate from oozing out between her lips.

I could see sheer terror on her face when Gavin started telling a joke and Sophie and I burst out laughing. Mat's eyes filled with tears and bits of melted chocolate started to dribble out the sides of her mouth. In a last desperate attempt to save face, she ran to the dam and dived in.

Unfortunately, she dived straight into another dead sheep and came up out of the dam screaming hysterically, waving a rotten sheep leg in her hand, and dribbling chocolate all down the front of her yellow bathers.

Peter and Gavin staggered around laughing.

After they'd gone, Sophie and I tried to console her.

'It wasn't that bad,' said Sophie. 'I'm sure he didn't notice anything odd.'

'And even if he did,' I said reassuringly, 'I'm certain he feels like you're dumber than him.'

Mat gave me one of those withering stares.

Sunday, 28 January

Petal is all grown up!

I accidentally shut her inside while I went to feed the chooks. She carried on like a pork chop until Mum opened the door for her. She ran straight off the edge of the veranda and *flew* to me! I caught her in my arms and she nibbled my ears with joy.

I'm so proud. Her first flight!

Mat and Sophie are both driving me nuts. They spent the day in the sleep-out, painting their toenails purple and going through Sophie's *Girl Alive* magazines. They were reading the Love Doctor letters — the ones where girls write in and say things like:

Dear Love Doctor,
My next-door neighbour is a fourteen-year-old spunk and even though he has a brain the size of a walnut, I am madly in love with him. The only trouble is he doesn't seem to know that I exist. What should I do?
Yours sincerely,
Shy Girl Next Door With A Brain The Size Of A Peanut

Sophie and I usually laugh ourselves stupid at them. But Mat was taking the letters really seriously. She said maybe *she* should write in and ask about her relationship problems with Gavin.

Relationship???

I told Mat she was such an expert on love that she should start her *own* Love Doctor column. She took it as a *compliment*. Good grief!

I went outside to muck around with Peter and

Gavin. We spent the afternoon shovelling sheep manure from under the shearing shed to put on Mum's garden. It turns out that Gavin is *fascinated* by poo. He has serious plans to start his own organic fertiliser company, using the vast quantities of unused poo lying around on farms. It sounds like a great idea, actually — environmentally friendly and money saving.

Mat, however, was not impressed when I told her. I pointed out that Gavin probably wouldn't have time to study the law if he was busy travelling the countryside, collecting enormous vats of poo.

She stared out the window for a long time, then said, 'Who cares? I never liked him anyway!'

Just like that!

Can it really have been love if a little bit of poop scares it away?

I JUST DON'T KNOW.

Monday, 29 January

Peter reminded us all at breakfast that, next week, he, Sophie and Gavin are returning to boarding school.

I hate boarding school. All it does is rip families apart and drag them away from the land where they belong.

At least *I'm* not being banished from Hillrose Poo. Mat, Ben Simpson and I will be starting our online tutoring for year seven at Hardbake Plains Public School. Thanks to three years of drought, no-one can afford to send more kids off to boarding school. This is obviously a *good* thing, but Matilda Jane the Mature thinks it's as devastating as global warming.

'Another year at Hardbake Plains with all those silly children will be *torture*,' she moaned. 'I need to get away from here or I'll die. You're so lucky, Sophie. Boarding school is as cool as.'

Yeah right! As cool as a poke in the eye with a blunt stick, or boils on your bum.

Wes and Fez brought the three-legged dead sheep from the dam home this afternoon.

'We've got big plans for her, Blue,' said Wes.

'Her name's Wendy,' said Fez.

As if that explains it!

Tuesday, 30 January

Mat, Sophie and I were climbing on the hay bales beside the driveway today when a big black car arrived. Out popped Miss McKenzie followed by MRS WELSH-PEARSON AND JAMES!!!

Sophie and Matilda Jane the Mature flew at them, squealing and blowing so many air kisses that I thought they might start a dust storm. Mum, the big fat traitor, invited them all inside for a cuppa.

James, Miss McKenzie and Mrs WP sipped tea. They laughed and chattered as though nothing in the world was wrong …

As though Miss McKenzie hadn't nearly cried herself to death with a broken heart …

As though James Welsh-Pearson wasn't the biggest doofus in the whole wide world …

AS THOUGH THE ENGAGEMENT HAD NEVER BEEN BROKEN OFF!!!

'Of *course* the wedding will be here at Hillrose Poo!' Mrs WP cried. 'It was all just a silly misunderstanding.'

'Katherine is the love of my life,' James declared.

Spew central! It was an absolute disaster and I was sick of listening to all the drivel — wedding, wedding, wedding, love, kissy, kissy, blah, blah, blah …

It would have gone on for hours if it wasn't for the Flying Ferals and their latest catapult stunt. Suddenly there was an enormous bang, as the dead sheep from the dam slammed against the

dining-room window. It slid slowly down the fly screen, leaving bits of decayed eyeball and maggoty wool behind as it went.

Sophie screamed and hid her face in the tablecloth. Mat started to retch and ran from the room. Mum sighed wearily and poured herself another cup of tea. James and Mrs WP stared in horror, speechless, and Miss McKenzie burst out laughing.

'That's Wendy, the Flying Ferals' new assistant,' I explained.

I went outside to congratulate the boys. I was elated. I thought *that* would be the end of it. I was ready to tell Wes and Fez that I love them and that they were the cleverest boys in the world for driving the Welsh-Pearsons away from Miss McKenzie FOREVER.

But they hadn't.

Half an hour later, James and Miss McKenzie left, arm in arm, making googly-goggle eyes at each other. Mrs WP followed behind, chatting to Mum and smiling. She didn't even snarl when Dad drove by in the ute, yelling, 'Hello Jacinta!'

And that's when I realised. The Welsh-Pearsons really *do* want Miss McKenzie to be part of their family and they will do *anything* to make sure it happens. And why wouldn't they? She is just wonderful and warm and cheerful and kind and generous. No-one would ever want her to walk out of their life once they had her there.

But she's going to walk out of *our* lives.

Soon.

What a lousy, rotten bummer of a day.

Wednesday, 31 January

Mat and Gavin have both gone home. Mat tried to leave without taking Sheba, but Mr Sweeney wouldn't let her. Hee, hee, hee!

Mum sat me down after they left and gave me a serious talking to.

'Miss McKenzie is a grown woman, Blue, and has to make her own decisions in life,' she said.

I rolled my eyes and tried to look unconvinced, but then Mum said, 'If we truly love Miss McKenzie, we will support her in whatever she chooses to do. We will also accept and love the people that she loves.'

She wasn't suggesting. She was telling.

I hate it when Mum does that.

February

Thursday, 1 February

Helped Wes and Fez bury Wendy down behind the old outdoor dunny. We made a little cross out of timber and I said a prayer.

Wes said she was the bravest three-legged circus sheep he had ever known.

Fez said she was the most acrobatically gifted sheep ever to have lived at Hillrose Poo, and burst into tears.

Friday, 2 February

Woken at 5 am by Gunther's squeals and snorts, and a high-pitched shriek which turned out to be coming from Macka. We ran out the back to see a fox disappear into the dark.

The ducks were quacking and flapping on top of the chook shed. Silly things must have flown up, but they couldn't get down again. Peter had to climb up and rescue them.

Gunther paced back and forth like an anxious mother, huffing and puffing until all three ducks were safely back with him on the veranda. He grunted gently and tucked them away between his fat body and the firewood box. Macka trotted back and forth on the grass, keeping watch.

Rotten foxes. I'm glad Macka the crazy alpaca is here to play bodyguard.

Mum took Sophie and Peter into Dubbo for the day to buy school stuff. I stayed home to help Dad weld a new gate for the shearing yard. I refuse to be part of something as horrible and destructive as setting children up for another year of boarding school.

Saturday, 3 February

Miss McKenzie, James and Mrs WP came out for lunch today. I was very supportive and smiled sweetly at everyone. I even gave Mrs WP an air kiss with a mega-loud *Mwaah*!

Mum scowled at me.

Miss McKenzie had her beautiful, curly, carroty hair pulled back into a tight bun so that you could hardly see it. Why would she want to do that? James kept tucking escaping frizzes back into the bun, saying, 'That's better.'

Mrs WP had to inspect the garden for the wedding. It looked beautiful — golden brown grass, an enormous shady peppercorn tree, and a view that stretched for miles across the dry, dusty plains. There were yellow flowers on the honeysuckle vine that grows over the chook shed, and creamy white blossoms on the gumtrees. I thought it was perfect, but Mrs WP had all sorts of ideas to make it *better* — potted plants, paved paths, avenues of pink roses ...

It would have all been incredibly boring if Macka hadn't appeared from nowhere and spat at Mrs WP. He lifted his top lip to show two ugly buckteeth and trotted away, gurgling happily.

Mrs WP's hat was dripping with green slimy goop. Mum wiped it clean with her apron and sat it on the veranda to dry. She said the hat would

be as good as new in no time, and it probably would have been if Gerty hadn't eaten it.

When Mrs WP left, her smile was so stiff that her face nearly cracked. I scratched Gerty behind the ear and told her she was a good girl.

Sunday, 4 February

Peter and Sophie leave tomorrow.

They spent the day helping Wes, Fez and me build a cubbyhouse in the peppercorn tree. We used an old machinery crate for the main part and built timber platforms on either side, staggered up the tree. It was all joined by ladders. It looked amazing — a bit wonky, but a real home-made tree cubby.

Mum brought dinner out so we could stay in our new house. She and Dad sat on a picnic blanket nearby with Macka, Doris, Gertrude and Mildred, listening to the cricket on the radio.

Sophie sat on the tree-house balcony and sighed, 'There's no place like home.'

I thought she was dreading going back to boarding school, but it turns out she's just sooky because she'll miss out on all the wedding preparations. She's made me promise to email her all the details!

I'm *dreading* the wedding preparations so much that I *almost* offered to go to boarding school in her place, but that would be like offering to give up the chance to have the flu for the opportunity to have the Black Plague.

Monday, 5 February

Well, they're gone. Dad drove Sophie and Peter away, down the driveway, out through the front gate of Hillrose Poo, away from the land where they belong.

And here I am, left with nothing to cheer me up except a packet of chocolate biscuits, Petal and the hope that Gunther will turn nasty and eat Wes and Fez alive before sundown.

Tuesday, 6 February

Spent the morning helping Wes and Fez organise their stuff for school. I covered twelve exercise books with contact, and stuck name labels on forty-eight pencils. Wes ironed two school shirts, a pair of shorts and fourteen pairs of undies while Fez arranged the lunchbox snacks in alphabetical order in the pantry. It was so weird — almost like they were trying to be helpful.

Matilda Jane the Mature rang after lunch to ask what I am wearing tomorrow!! The year sevens aren't officially at school because of our online learning, so we don't need to be in uniform. Before I could even begin to think about whether I'd wear my new blue shorts or my old blue shorts, Mat described her whole outfit — a denim skirt and white T-shirt with love hearts on the front, four different types of bangles, red and blue cotton scarf, red ballerina-style shoes with silver studs on the straps and matching red hair band!!!

I told her that I was a little bit concerned that she hadn't chosen a necklace. She let out a scream of shock, thanked me *so much* for reminding her, and hung up.

She's obviously gone to search for the perfect necklace but, really, she should be spending the afternoon searching for a brain.

Wednesday, 7 February

Back to school today. Left Petal sobbing behind the kitchen door.

Wes drove the old ute down to the bus stop and didn't even speed, skid or side-swipe any trees on the way. He said he was turning over a new leaf, now that he was going into year three.

'I'm gonna be mature, Blue,' he said seriously. 'I've gotta be a good example for Fez.'

Fez grinned at me. He was wearing Grandpa Weston's old false teeth, which he'd found in the back of the kitchen dresser last night. He looked like buck-toothed Macka.

Mat, Ben, Banjo and I sat down the back of the bus and tried to have an intelligent conversation. It wasn't easy. Matilda Jane's bangles were jangling so much, I could hardly hear Ben talking about his trip to his cousin's house.

Miss McKenzie and Mr Cluff were waiting to greet the bus when we arrived at school. Miss

McKenzie looked as happy and sparkly as ever, although she was wearing very dull clothes and had her hair in a bun again. Mr Cluff looked like he'd just cut his hair with a carving knife.

Mr Cluff led Ben, Mat and me straight into the little study nook off the senior classroom, where our computers were all set up. He spent the first half-hour showing us how to log on to different sites and connect with other students, and left us a choice of activities to do for the week. We felt so grown-up in our own room without a teacher.

After recess we joined the rest of the school for a start-of-year assembly. There are three new kindergarten kids: Lucy Ferris's sister, Cassie; Sarah Love's brother, James; and Harry Wilson's sister, Dora. They all looked so proud to be at school and they all love Miss McKenzie. By the time Mr Cluff had finished his pep talk, Dora and James had fallen asleep on her lap and Cassie was twirling a piece of Miss McKenzie's frizzy red hair around her finger.

Banjo pointed out that Mr Cluff looked like *he* would like to be twirling a piece of Miss McKenzie's hair around *his* finger! Is he serious???

At lunch time Mat and I sat together on the steps, laughing at James Love. He's so cute and tiny but has a lunchbox the size of an Esky. He stayed at the picnic table for three-quarters of an hour and ate two cheese salad sandwiches, an apple, a banana and a muesli bar. He'd already eaten two lamingtons, a packet of chips and an orange at recess. He started to cry when the bell went because he hadn't found time to drink his chocolate milk. Gary Hartley has nicknamed him Worms, because he eats so much but stays so skinny.

By home time, Mat had sent four emails to a year seven boy out the back of Warren and was totally in love. Ben and I had used *our* time to do the week's lessons on division, research the three levels of government in Australia, and partner-read the first chapter of our novel, *Dusty Dreams*. It was kind of cool having our own space to work, but I miss being in with the other kids.

Petal was so excited to see me when I got home. She flew off the veranda, straight into my arms and covered me with duck-nibbles. What a cutie!

Thursday, 8 February

Mat actually did some work today, once she'd emailed Warren three times to see what subjects he was focusing on.

I was a bit confused and asked if he was *called* Warren or *from* Warren. Mat blushed and said both. Ben and I burst out laughing, so she wouldn't talk to us for the rest of the day.

Lucy, Cassie, Banjo and I sat in the shade at lunch time playing with Lucy's bunnies. Banjo stared at Mr Cluff as he walked across the playground to Miss McKenzie.

'Watch,' said Banjo.

Mr Cluff put his hand on her shoulder and his eyes looked so terribly gentle. Just like Gunther looks when his ducks give him nibbley kisses on the snout. As Miss McKenzie walked away to the staffroom, his shoulders sagged and he sighed.

I felt guilty. Like I'd peeped through someone's window and seen them picking their nose and wiping it on the sofa. We weren't meant to see Mr Cluff's feelings like this.

I pointed out that Worms had already eaten two ham sandwiches, an orange, a pear and a tub of strawberry yoghurt.

Banjo seemed cross that I'd changed the topic.

'Mr Cluff can't help feeling that way,' he said. 'If you love someone, you just love them.'

Love?

Mr Cluff?? Miss McKenzie???

Is Banjo for real???

Why does everyone get this love stuff except me???

Friday, 9 February

Mrs Whittington is glad that the school term has started. She missed seeing and hearing all the hustle and bustle of kids in the schoolyard.

Today she came over at recess with a steamed golden syrup pudding and gave it to Worms, saying, 'I've finally made that pudding that I promised you, Blue. Lovely essay, darling. The bush is the heart of our beautiful country. Well done. Well done. Enjoy the pudding.'

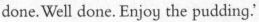

Worms's eyes nearly popped out of his head. He couldn't believe his luck. He had no idea why Mrs Whittington was giving him a whole steamed golden syrup pudding, or why she was calling him Blue, but he smiled up at her, gave her a hug and took the pudding. He sat down at the picnic table and ploughed his way through it.

Mrs Whittington sat down beside Worms and watched. She smiled and patted him on the head from time to time.

I was pretty disappointed that Worms got *my* golden syrup pudding, but he and Mrs Whittington both looked so happy. I could hardly interfere.

School newsletter day today. Mat was flapping the community notices page in my face as soon as we sat down on the bus to go home.

Dear Love Mechanic
New relationship advice column
starting here next week.
Send all your problems to:
The Love Mechanic
c/- Hardbake Plains Public School
Barnes Rd
Hardbake Plains
Remember, there's no problem too big or small
for the Love Mechanic to solve.

MATILDA JANE THE MATURE IS THE LOVE MECHANIC.

What a tragedy.

And it's all my fault!

Saturday, 10 February

Woken at 5 am by Gunther's snorting and Macka's screaming. The ducks were quacking and flapping on top of the chicken coop. Two foxes hung around behind the old outdoor dunny then slipped away into the dark. They're getting cheeky.

Mum had to climb onto the chicken coop and pass the ducks down to Dad. Gunther hid them behind the firewood box. Macka continued to trot around the back yard, his ears pulled back and his eyes rolling so that you could see the whites. He looked crazy angry.

Wes and Fez have carpeted the tree house. It looks great and is really comfy to sit on.

Sunday, 11 February

Today at Mass, Father O'Malley talked about the part in the Bible where it says, 'Greater love has no man than this — that he lay down his life for his friends.'

That must be proper love — the absolute best.

Gunther has that kind of love for his ducks. I know he'd die saving them from the foxes if he had to. And I think Macka would do the same for Gunther. Mum and Dad would lay down their life for us kids. That's just what mums and dads do. Even Wes and Fez would die for each other. They are completely feral, but they love each other heaps.

But what about James Welsh-Pearson? Would he throw himself in front of Miss McKenzie to shield her from gunfire? Would he dive into a raging river to save her from drowning? Would he run into a burning building, risking his own life to save hers?

I asked Mat what she thought. Her eyes glazed over and she sighed, 'How *totally* romantic.' I think the whole point was lost inside her attractively small brain.

I'm not so sure. If James loves Miss McKenzie so much, why does he want her to change? If you won't let someone play the bagpipes, or laugh when they snort chocolate mousse out their nose, or let their wild, carroty hair frizz out

in the breeze, you're hardly going to leap in front
of a train to save them, are you?

But what would I know?

Monday, 12 February
Asked Banjo about the Greatest Love thing
today. He sighed. He sounded like Matilda Jane
the Mature!!!

Later on in the day I found this poem sitting
beside my computer:

How deep is love?
As deep as the deepest sea?
As deep as the Grand Canyon?
As deep as a puddle of wee?

How long does love last?
As long as a summer or spring?
As long as a whole lifetime?
As long as a piece of string?

How sweet is love?
As sweet as a mountain stream?
As sweet as butterfly kisses?
As sweet as pudding and cream?

How true is love?
As true as an oath in court?
As true as Wikipedia?
As true as a fading thought?

Is *this* his answer to my question about how much James loves Miss McKenzie? And if it is, does he think James loves her as deeply as the Grand Canyon or as deeply as a puddle of wee?

Tuesday, 13 February

Fez has started wearing Grandpa Weston's glasses to school because he thinks they make him look smart. They don't.

He can't see properly through the thick, scratched lenses and he keeps bumping into things. He knocked Lynette Sweeney over twice today. The second time, Nick Farrel grabbed him by the front of the shirt and was about to punch his lights out but Wes convinced him it was wrong to hit a person with glasses.

Some of the kids have been asking Mr Cluff about outdoor projects. They are the best thing about school.

Last year we had some great stuff happening. Harry Wilson set out to dig to China and trapped a criminal instead. Sam Wotherspoon kept half the district fed with giant zucchinis, which was very helpful during the drought. Mrs Murphy even came up with a new zucchini chocolate cake recipe that won the CWA National Cake Baking Competition in Wagga Wagga. Lucy learnt all about multiplication from her two rabbits who ended up having dozens of babies.

But none of that seems to matter to Mr Cluff. He said we might have to wait a while because he's too busy to get organised. Then he sat down on the veranda steps and chatted with Miss McKenzie for the rest of lunch.

Matilda Jane the Mature is already totally engrossed in her own special project. The Love Mechanic received her first letter today:

Dear Love Mechanic,
My dad's truck has broken down and it's a damned nuisance because we are still only halfway through carting our wheat to the railway silos. Can you please come and help us fix it?
Ned Murphy

Ben and I nearly died laughing, but Mat was a bit disappointed. She's hoping for a more romantic problem before Friday.

Wednesday, 14 February — Valentine's Day

Everyone at school received wedding invitations today. On Saturday, 31 March, Miss McKenzie becomes Mrs Katherine Isobel Welsh-Pearson. Matilda Jane the Over-enthusiastic Bridesmaid was ecstatic and declared that this was the most romantic Valentine's Day ever!

Miss McKenzie said that we all have to be her family because only a few of her real family can come out from Scotland for the wedding.

The whole school was bustling with excitement. Lucy promised Miss McKenzie a pair of her prettiest bunnies as a wedding present. Sam Wotherspoon has already started composting around his latest golden squash plant so that he can give the bride and groom the world's largest vegetable ever. Harry Wilson said he will take Miss McKenzie and James to Greenland for their honeymoon if his hot air balloon is finished in time.

Gabby Woodhouse offered to give everyone a special haircut before the big day, and ran off to practise on Dora Wilson. Dora now has a crew cut just like Harry's and they look like twins. Dora is quite pleased.

So I suppose projects are starting with or without Mr Cluff's help ...

The Love Mechanic received two more envelopes today. The first one was Cassie Ferris's lunch order for two party pies with sauce, a custard tart and a carton of strawberry milk. But the second one contained a proper letter:

Dear Love Mechanic,
Can you please tell Santa that the bike he gave me for Christmas was the wrong one? I wanted the red one not the blue one.
Yours sincerely,
Cheesed Off

I think the Love Mechanic was pretty cheesed off, too. It can't be easy being a delicate genius in a world of idiots.

Thursday, 15 February

Wes and Fez are being suspiciously quiet. Other than cutting out the carpet from under their beds for the tree house, they have been incredibly well behaved. Wes is sitting up the front of the classroom and works like a professor all day long. He even studies at night. He's taking this whole year three maturity thing a little bit too seriously.

Fez isn't doing much work at all but he is trying very hard to look intelligent in Grandpa Weston's glasses. He has also started wearing a tie to school and carries four different pens tucked into his shirt pocket.

What are they up to?

Mat told me I should just enjoy the peace and quiet while it lasts, but she just doesn't get it. It's unnatural. If they squash their true natures for too long, it will burst out in some dreadful, destructive way sooner or later. I just know it.

Mrs Whittington brought Worms another steamed golden syrup pudding at lunch time today. She was wearing a red bathing suit and a swimming cap covered in white rubber flowers. Worms didn't mind. He gave her a big hug, took the pudding and the spoon, and ploughed his way through. Mrs Whittington sat beside him, saying, 'Lovely essay, dear. The bush is the heart of our beautiful country.'

Friday, 16 February

The Love Mechanic had her first real column published in the school newsletter today. Well, it wasn't real at all actually. Mat ended up writing the letter herself. She didn't think Cassie Ferris's lunch order really set the right tone …

Here it is:

Dear Love Mechanic,

My best friend and I are both totally in love with the same boy. The boy is obviously more interested in me than he is in my friend. I am, like, *so much* prettier. Anyway, I am worried that my friend will totally hate my guts if I become this boy's girlfriend. We have been friends, like, forever. What should I do?

Yours sincerely,

Pretty but Confused

And as if *that* wasn't scary enough, *this* was the Love Mechanic's reply:

Dear Pretty but Confused,
Love is a complicated and beautiful thing. Ditch your best friend and become this boy's girlfriend. You have had a lifetime of fun and support from your friend. Now it's time to have fun with someone else. Being this boy's girlfriend is far more important and will make you look so totally cool. Yours sincerely,
The Love Mechanic

What sort of advice is this??? I might not be an expert on love, but I really don't think this is the right answer. Thank goodness Pretty but Confused is a figment of Matilda Jane's imagination!

Caught Wes and Fez flicking through my bridesmaid's scrapbook this evening.

'Weddings are very special, Blue,' said Wes.

'And important,' said Fez.

'You're very lucky to be a bridesmaid, Blue,' said Wes.

'And important,' said Fez, and he burst out crying.

What does it all mean?????

Saturday, 17 February

We are all heartbroken.

We were woken at 4.30 this morning by Gunther and Macka. Gunther was running back and forth along the fence near the old pit dunny, squealing and frothing at the mouth. He kept trying to squeeze through the gaps in the wire. Poor thing was bleeding from little cuts all over his back.

Macka was running around in circles, rolling his eyes, shrieking and spitting. Fluffles was on top of the clothesline, puffed up to five times her usual size, her eyes as big as saucers.

Dad, Wes and Fez grabbed the torches and wandered across the paddocks looking for the ducks. Mum and I searched all over the house yard and around the sheds, but they were nowhere to be seen.

By the time the sun came up we all knew that the three ducks had been taken by foxes. Gunther flopped down on the veranda, near the firewood box. He put his big, fat head on the floor and moaned. Gerty, Doris and Mildred lay down either side of Gunther and grunted softly. Macka stood on the grass nearby and hummed.

Wes, Fez and I all began to cry.

Poor little ducks.

Poor Gunther.

We held a memorial service this afternoon, down beside Wendy's grave. We placed a little plaque on the dirt — a rock that Fez had written on:

Three ducks
Loved by Gunther
RIP

Mum made a little wreath of rosemary which Wes and Fez lay beside the plaque.

Gunther lay on the veranda all day. He didn't move. He didn't even eat.

Sunday, 18 February

Gunther lay under the peppercorn tree all day, surrounded by Macka, Gertrude, Doris and Mildred. Macka hummed soothingly, stopping every now and then to nuzzle Gunther's head or neck.

It breaks your heart when someone you love dies.

Gunther's heart must have broken three times over.

Monday, 19 February

Harry Wilson is bringing bags of fabric to school each day. He's going to sew it all together for his hot air balloon. Davo Hartley has promised to bring in his mum's sewing machine to help. Tom Gillies has promised to bring in his mum's laundry basket for the passengers to ride in.

None of us know what to do about Gunther's grief. He's still not eating or moving.

Gerty brought him a piece of bread from her slops bowl this morning, but he wouldn't even sniff it. Gerty never *ever* shares her food with anyone. She must love him very much to be so concerned.

Wes and Fez spent the afternoon lying in the shade with the pigs. Fez scratched Gunther behind the ear and he just groaned. He didn't bare his teeth or look like he wanted to rip Fez to shreds. It was heartbreaking.

I've never seen anyone so miserable.

Tuesday, 20 February

AAAAAGH!!!

I've had a very stressful day. Mum started it by telling me that James Welsh-Pearson is arriving tomorrow. He's staying at Hillrose Poo.

Matilda Jane the Most Important Bridesmaid Ever to Have Walked the Earth was hyper-ventilating about James's visit because it means that there will be more WEDDING PREPARATIONS going on. She kept hinting that she should sleep over at Hillrose Poo, but I pretended I had an ear infection and couldn't hear what she was saying.

Miss McKenzie is so excited about James's visit that her brain has turned to porridge and all she can do is blush and giggle. Mr Cluff sat beside her all lunch time and blushed and giggled too!

Then Banjo popped up from nowhere and gave me this poem!!!

Mr C loves Miss McK –
I've seen it in his eyes.
When Miss McK sits near at lunch,
He shoos away her flies.

When Miss McK forgets her fruit,
He shares his last banana.
And often brings her little snacks,
Like cheese sticks and cabana.

When she brings the bagpipes out,
His face lights up with joy.
And when she says his name out loud,
He giggles like a boy.

When Miss McK walks through the yard,
He gazes from afar.
And when she walks into the room,
He holds the door ajar.

When Miss McK is late for school,
He paces to and fro.
And when she leaves at 5 pm,
His shoulders sag down low.

It's obvious that Mr C
Thinks Miss McK is hot.
It's just a shame that Miss McK
Thinks Mr C is not!

This is all so confusing. I think we just need to put a ban on love for a while. Things are getting out of control around here.

My head was spinning by the time I got home, so I took Petal down to the dam for a swim.

Gunther still hasn't moved or eaten. I wonder how long pigs can go without food before they die.

Wednesday, 21 February

James Welsh-Pearson is here.

He called into the school and spent the afternoon helping Miss McKenzie in the junior classroom. I thought he'd be worried about getting glitter glue or sticky fingerprints on his fancy suit, but he seemed quite happy in there ... until Worms vomited his lunch all over James's shoes.

Good old Worms and his salmon sandwiches.

James was going to drive us home in his big, silver four-wheel drive, but made some lame excuse at the last minute about waiting behind to bring Miss McKenzie to our place for dinner. I think he just got scared when he saw Fez grinning stupidly through his false teeth and bug-eyed glasses.

Dinner was agony. Miss McKenzie had her hair in that ugly bun and was wearing the most boring brown dress I have ever seen. She used to look so colourful and interesting. Worst of all, she had covered her beautiful freckles with make-up so that you couldn't see a single spot. I felt totally betrayed as I sat there eating my roast lamb with freckles all over my wide nose.

Dad asked James how Jacinta was going. James said Jacinta was a cow and Dad said that was no way to talk about his mother. Wes and Fez were being so well behaved that even Miss McKenzie was getting edgy. And, just as dessert was served, Petal flew onto the table and did a poo on my bread and butter plate. James was not impressed.

Actually, Mum wasn't impressed either.

Sophie rang after dinner and screeched when I told her James was visiting. She started asking all about what he had said and done and what car he drove and what he was wearing and what he had eaten. I asked if she wanted me to ring when he went to the toilet, and did she want to know whether it was number ones or number twos? That's when she decided she'd talk to Mum.

Thursday, 22 February

James Welsh-Pearson called in at school for recess.

Mat hung around like a bad smell until Wes and Fez dragged her away, suggesting that Miss McKenzie might want some special time alone with her fiancé. Things have really gone out of whack when Wes and Fez are teaching Matilda Jane how to be mature!!!!

Mrs Whittington came over with a steamed golden syrup pudding. She was wearing her red bathers, yellow gumboots and the Miss Wool and Wheat sash over her shoulder. James's eyes nearly popped out of his head.

Mrs Whittington shouted at James:
'Sticky stare, like a bear,
Like a sausage in the air.
When the sausage busted,
You fell in the custard.
When your mother came in
She was disgusted.'

She gave Worms the pudding and stomped off home.

Everyone burst out laughing. Everyone except James, that is.

Serves him right. It's rude to stare. Mrs Whittington was only delivering a gift. His mother should have brought him up better.

Gunther still isn't eating. Dad is getting quite concerned and said Gunther might need some professional help.

I just hope he doesn't write to the Love Mechanic!

Friday, 23 February

Saw the best thing ever when we got home from school. Gunther was lying under the peppercorn tree, with three tiny, white, fluffy baby bunnies tucked up between his front legs. He was grunting softly and nuzzling them with his big, fat snout. He was as happy as a kookaburra at a snake farm.

That explains why Mr Sweeney bought three of Lucy's baby bunnies at lunch time today. It wasn't for rabbit stew after all!

The Love Mechanic had her first *real* relationship problem published today:

Dear Love Mechanic,
There's a girl at school who keaps giving me werms. Duz this meen she loves me?
Yours sinsearly,
Confused

The reply was:

Dear Confused,
Love is a complicated and beautiful thing. We probably need to be clear on the type of worms that you are being given. If they are slimy pink earthworms for your compost heap, then they are obviously gifts given with thought. This girl knows how important compost is for growing giant vegetables, and wants to help you in any way she can. This is love.

If however they are the type of worms that make you skinny and set your bum itching, I don't think it is love. You probably need to see your local doctor (or vet) about some tablets. You also need to ask the girl to wash her hands thoroughly with soap and water before coming near you or your compost heap.

Yours sincerely,

The Love Mechanic

Great advice!

Rang Mat to congratulate her, but she wouldn't talk. Miss McKenzie and James were there for dinner and she didn't want to miss out on *anything*.

Just when I think that girl has grown a brain it vanishes once more ...

Saturday, 24 February

Miss McKenzie is a traitor!

I can barely believe it.

I overheard Mum, Dad, Miss McKenzie and James talking about Mrs Whittington.

Mrs Whittington can't live alone because of her Alzheimer's. When James marries Miss McKenzie and takes her away from Hardbake Plains, Mrs Whittington will be all alone. Her son, Bob, will send her back to the nursing home and she hates it there. She just wants to be at home, where the sun is hot and the plains stretch out for miles ... Where she can have her own chooks and vegie patch ... Where she can cook her own meals and choose which clothes to wear — even if they *are* bathers and gumboots … Where everyone loves her and accepts her as she is … Where she BELONGS.

But Miss McKenzie has other plans.

I heard her saying something about a *home* and *relocating*.

And I heard Mum and Dad agree.

Worst of all, I heard James say, 'Super! That's a jolly good idea.'

Everyone is talking about James and Miss McKenzie and all the love. What about showing Mrs Whittington some love? Isn't love looking after people? Taking care of them? Doing what is BEST for them???

Sunday, 25 February

Miss McKenzie isn't a traitor after all. She's a genius!

Dad, James and Mr Murphy spent the day building a chicken coop at the back of the shearers' cottage. Mum and Miss McKenzie cleaned inside the cottage and painted the kitchen bright yellow. They painted the front door blue and changed the sign on the wall so it no longer says Serenity Cottage. It's now called Magpie's Rest. Just like Mrs Whittington's house.

Mrs Whittington is moving to Hillrose Poo! The idea is to make her new home as similar to her old home as possible. That way she might not get so confused with the change. Tomorrow all her furniture and stuff will be moved in. Her chooks will be brought to the identical chicken coop. Miss McKenzie will even live there until she gets married!

The only problem is that our house will be where the school usually sits, but Mum said we will help Mrs Whittington cope with that somehow or other.

She won't be able to stay here forever. Her Alzheimer's *will* get worse. But until then, us Westons will gladly keep an eye on her!

Now *that* is love.

Monday, 26 February

Miss McKenzie and Mrs Whittington are here at Hillrose Poo, living in Magpie's Rest! James, Mum and Dad moved their things over today.

Mrs Whittington doesn't seem to mind the change. She fed her chooks and locked them up after dinner. Then she sat in a rocking chair on her veranda and had a lovely chat with Gertrude, Doris and Mildred. She didn't even seem to think there was anything out of place when 'Ugly, Ugly, Ugly World' by Festering Punks was blasted across the plains and Gerty started banging her head against the wall.

James gave everyone farewell presents tonight. He drives back to Sydney in the morning. He gave Mum a Beethoven CD, which she can't ever play because Gerty would go psycho, and gave Dad a silk tie. Wes and Fez got a DVD called *Circus Blitz* — a new Australian circus that James has done some legal work for. Mum slipped it between the dictionary and the Bible on the bookshelf when she thought no-one was looking.

James gave me a silver heart-shaped photo frame.

Who does he think I am? Matilda Jane the Bridesmaid?

Tuesday, 27 February

Wes and Fez were up early this morning. They made cups of tea and about twelve pieces of toast for James. Wes made James's bed while Fez polished his shoes. Then they stood side by side on the driveway, waving like little angels, as he drove away. It was terrifying.

But the minute James was gone, Wes said a lot of *very* bad words that I would not even write. Fez ripped his tie off and trampled it in the dirt. He took the pens out of his shirt pocket and snapped them in half one by one. He pulled Grandpa Weston's glasses off and threw them at Doris.

I *knew* the twin tornadoes couldn't keep up the goody-two-shoes act!

Fez said there was no point in being well behaved. It was boring as boogers and people still didn't make you into bridesmaids. Wes said Fez was a sissy pink-pants and that boys got made into pageboys not bridesmaids. Fez said they were both too stupid to get made into *anything* for Miss McKenzie's wedding and Wes had a stinky poo brain and an ugly maggot face. Then they started hitting and kicking each other and rolling around in the dust.

Mrs Whittington stood on the veranda of Magpie's Rest and yelled, 'Get on in to school you naughty little boys!'

Wes and Fez spent half the school day wearing tea cosies on their heads, chasing kids around the yard and whacking them with Sam's giant zucchinis. They spent the other half of the day in detention writing apology letters to Mr Cluff for calling him a wombat's bum and to Miss McKenzie for calling her a freckle-faced chook.

What a relief! It is just *so good* to have the real Wes and Fez back.

Wednesday, 28 february

Mat showed me a very disturbing Love Mechanic letter today.

Dear Love Mechanic,

I am madly in love with a girl at my school. She is in year seven, is really smart and has red hair. Some kids say her face looks like it is covered in fly spots, but I adore her freckles. They make her nose look like it's been kissed by hundreds of fairies.

She does not know that I am in love with her. I am only in year five. Should I tell her my feelings or should I suffer in silence?

Yours sincerely,

Poet in Agony

Oh man! Banjo is such a doofus.

And who says my face looks like it's covered in fly spots???

I made Mat promise not to use it for this week's Love Mechanic column.

The Flying Ferals found the *Circus Blitz* DVD this afternoon. It fell out of its hiding spot in the bookshelf when Fez grabbed the dictionary to hit Wes over the head. They spent hours watching it with Mrs Whittington.

Fez kept replaying this freaky section with a contortionist. First the contortionist slipped his whole body through a tennis racket by dislocating his arms and hips and becoming all rubbery. Then he stuck his legs behind his head (yucko!) and squeezed into a little glass box.

Mrs Whittington sat on the lounge, clutching a steamed golden syrup pudding to her chest. I think she had brought it over for Worms, then forgot about it when she couldn't find him. She took it home with her three hours later. Bummer.

March

Thursday, 1 March

This morning when Petal and I went out to collect the eggs before school, Gunther was lying on his back as the bunnies hopped all over his belly. He was making a weird sneezing sound which I think might have been laughter. Macka stood nearby and gurgled happily. So cute!

Thought I'd better face Banjo about the Love Mechanic letter today. He said it wasn't him, but I pointed out that he is the only poet in year five. So then he said he loves me. I told him it was probably just indigestion.

I think we both felt better after our little chat. Maybe I'm getting better at understanding love.

Fez got a tennis racket stuck around his shoulders at lunch time. He had to wear it all afternoon until Mr Ferris arrived with his angle grinder and cut it off.

Friday, 2 March

This morning when Petal and I went out to collect the eggs before school, Wes was stuck in one of the nesting boxes! He was scrunched up in a little ball with his knees around his ears and his chin squished down on his chest. His eyes were popping out of his head. Fez was laughing his guts out.

Dad had to pull the front off the nesting box before Wes could get out and go to school.

Got a bit of a shock when I read the school newsletter this afternoon:

Dear Love Mechanic,

I am madly in love with a girl at my school. She is in year seven, is really smart and has red hair and freckles.

I have confessed my love to her, but she says it is probably just indigestion. What should I do?

Yours sincerely,

Poet in Agony

The reply was:

Dear Poet in Agony,

Love is a complicated and beautiful thing. Indigestion, on the other hand, is a complicated and ugly thing. It is important that you learn to recognise the difference between the two. Do you burp a lot and have a burning feeling in your tummy? Then it is probably indigestion. Do you sigh a lot and have a burning feeling in your heart? Then it is probably love.

If it is love, bad luck. There's *no way* a year seven girl would fall in love with a little year five boy. That would just be lame. But great poets often write about broken hearts, so suck it up and get writing.

Yours sincerely,
The Love Mechanic

Oh brother!

Saturday, 3 March

Fez got the wooden toilet seat from the old pit dunny stuck around his shoulders today. Wes was laughing so much as he sawed him free that he cut Fez's ear.

Mum bandaged him up and told him he looked like Vincent Van Gogh. Now Wes and Fez

think Vincent Van Gogh was a famous contortionist who cut off his ear so that he could fit into small places more easily.

Later on I heard them discussing cutting Wes's arms and legs off so that he could fit into the pigs' slops bucket. Nice!

Sunday, 4 March

Wes got his legs stuck behind his head this morning. He was rolling around on the grass in a tangled ball. Macka ran around him gurgling merrily. Fez offered to cut Wes's ears off so that his legs could slip forward again, but Mum wouldn't let him. Fez said it wasn't fair — Vincent Van Gogh's mother would have let him do it!

It took Mum and Miss McKenzie a quarter of an hour to get Wes unstuck without dislocating his hips.

I spent the afternoon helping Mrs Whittington sort out her wedding dress, pearls and veil. The wedding dress is so old that the sleeves are falling off and it's yellow around the hem. Mrs Whittington was quite upset that she couldn't find her bouquet, so I made one from lavender and geraniums. It looked pretty scruffy but she was happy.

She sat in her rocking chair for the rest of the day, holding the flowers and explaining to Gertrude, Doris and Mildred what their bridesmaid duties are.

I told Mum. She said Mrs Whittington is getting a bit confused by all the talk about Miss McKenzie's wedding.

Join the club!

I wonder if Gerty can do the bridesmaid's walk better than me ...

Monday, 5 March

Looks like Banjo listened to the Love Mechanic. Found this stuck to my computer screen when I arrived at school:

My words of love are spoken
But now my heart is broken.
It's bleeding like a scab that has been picked
    off before the sore is ready to heal.
How miserable I feel.

Wow! Intense!

And what happened in the middle there? If Banjo is going to write feral poems about love, they should at least have a decent rhythm.

Showed Mat. She sighed and said, 'How romantic.'

I don't think there's *anything* romantic about picking scabs until they bleed. But what would I know?

There were piles of sand and gravel and pavers all over the back yard when we got home. By the time dinner was ready, Wes, Fez and I had paved a full patio underneath the tree house. It looks great.

Tuesday, 6 March

Fez stayed home today. He got stuck in the blanket drawer in the bottom of his wardrobe before school and we had to leave before Mum could get him out.

This was taped to my computer screen when I arrived at school:

My heart is shrinking
Like an apple in the sun,
Like an overdried apricot,
Like a dehydrated plum.

I think someone's *brain* is shrinking …

Mrs Whittington was sitting on a deck chair under the peppercorn tree, when we got home. Mum said she'd been watching Gunther and his bunnies all afternoon.

When I brought Mrs Whittington a cup of tea, she said Gunther was the biggest, ugliest rabbit she had ever seen. I had to agree.

Wednesday, 7 March

This was stuck to my computer screen today:

My love is weak.
It used to be strong.
It's fading fast.
It can't go on.
My heart is empty.
My head is sore.
I don't want to
Love you no more.

What a relief! Maybe the Poet in Agony will turn back into good old Banjo by the end of the term.

Maybe he'll even sort his grammar out!

Then I'll just have Matilda Jane the Over-enthusiastic Bridesmaid and Miss McKenzie the Mush-Brained Bride-To-Be to deal with.

Mush-Brain McKenzie reminded Mat and me at recess that there are ONLY TWENTY-FOUR DAYS UNTIL THE WEDDING!!

Mat is ecstatic and spent her entire maths session emailing every online student she knows with the thrilling news. Warren from Warren emailed back with a little heart that danced across the screen. Mat nearly fainted with joy.

Ben stuck his finger down his throat at *exactly* the same time as me. Synchronised chundering! How cool was that?!!

Thursday, 8 March

Banjo is back to normal.

Just like that!

He sat next to me on the bus this morning and talked about Sam Wotherspoon's giant golden squash like nothing had ever happened.

I was a bit offended actually. How can he love me so much one minute and then not at all the next? Must be a shrinking heart or dried apricots or something.

Hope it's nothing to do with the fly spots on my nose …

Harry and Davo have sewn an enormous amount of material together for Harry's hot air balloon. They spread it out on the grass today and it reached halfway across the soccer field. Amazing.

Friday, 9 March

School newsletter day — the Love Mechanic strikes again:

Dear Love Mechanic,

There's this girl at my school called Lynette. You know how when people really don't like someone they say they hate their guts? Well I like Lynette so much that I *love* her guts. I want to get a tattoo on my arm that says I LOVE LYNETTE'S GUTS, but I'm not sure whether to have it written in a heart or a pile of guts. Which one is the most sensible?

Yours sincerely,

Tattoo Boy

The reply was:

Dear Tattoo Boy,
You can't say you love someone's guts. That's just gross. And it's totally stupid.

Besides, this girl Lynette sounds like she comes from a lovely family who probably hate tattoos. Why don't you just leave her alone and go get a maggot tattooed on your bum.
Yours sincerely,
The Love Mechanic

Mrs Whittington brought Gunther a steamed golden syrup pudding this afternoon. She placed it in front of him and said, 'Lovely essay, darling. The bush is the heart of our beautiful country. Well done.'

She sat on the grass and played with the baby bunnies while Gunther scoffed down the pudding.

Gunther doesn't usually let anyone near his baby bunnies, except for Uncle Macka the alpaca.

Saturday, 10 March — Wedding Working Bee

Mrs Clarissa Welsh-Pearson is here and she is staying in my bedroom!

160

She arrived at 8.30 am and had Macka's green goop dripping down her cheek by 8.31 am. She was not amused.

She didn't see the funny side of Wes running around with the toilet seat wedged over his shoulders and a bucket stuck over his head either, and it really *was* funny. Especially when he ran into the clothesline and knocked himself over.

The Sweeneys arrived at nine with Princess Lynette and Princess Matilda Jane.

By three o'clock, Mrs WP and Mrs Sweeney had ripped up our paving under the tree house and painted the chook shed, the old pit dunny and the laundry white. Dad and Mr Sweeney had paved little paths all over the back yard. Miss McKenzie and I had cleaned the veranda and pruned the rosemary. Mat and Lynette had fluttered their eyelids so much that all of their eyelashes had fallen out. And Mrs Whittington had fed Gertrude, Mildred and Doris the sponge cake, the scones and the raspberry coconut slice that Mum had baked for afternoon tea.

Thankfully, Miss McKenzie took Mrs WP to Hardbake Plains Pub for dinner tonight.

Mrs Whittington ate with us. She spent the whole evening talking about how excited she was about her engagement to Harold. Harold is her husband who died nine years ago.

Sunday, 11 March

Clarissa Welsh-Pearson and Sunshine got on like a house on fire last night. Mrs WP says Sunshine is a charming gentleman! Sunshine is the grumpiest old toad this side of the Black Stump.

Sunshine rang Dad this morning and said Mrs WP is a corker of a sheila!

This just proves that there's no explaining love.

Told Mat about Sunshine at Mass. She wouldn't believe me and said I should be ashamed of myself, lying in church.

Miss McKenzie has changed so much. She spent the afternoon working quietly beside Mrs WP in the garden, planting pink roses and tiny hedges. Miss McKenzie never used to be quiet. She used to talk all the time in her lovely Scottish lilt. Even when she had nothing much to say.

This afternoon Wes and Fez asked if she wanted a race in the pig chariots and she said no thank you. Miss McKenzie used to *love* racing through the dust in the pig chariots and didn't mind if she crashed or tipped over.

Then, when Macka appeared from nowhere and spat in her hair, she ran inside to clean up. The old Miss McKenzie would have rolled around on the grass laughing like a hyena.

She doesn't laugh out loud much any more, she just giggles, and when she smiles her eyes don't wrinkle and smile with her mouth. Her hair is always pulled back in a bun and she hasn't worn anything orange or purple or tie-dyed for ages. I haven't even *seen* the bagpipes. I thought she might start playing again once she moved back to Hillrose Poo, but she hasn't.

Talked to Mum about it this evening. Mum said love means give and take. Sometimes we have to change our lives to get along with the person we love. Like her and Dad. Dad takes off his dirty work boots before he comes inside, and tries not to curse too much, because he loves her. Mum gave up her job as a librarian to come and live on the farm because she loves Dad.

I pointed out that neither Mum nor Dad want to change the deep-down guts of who the other is. Boots and curses are just on the surface — same as whether you're in a library or in an ancient farmhouse. Mum is still a bookworm and Dad is still a grotty farmer.

James is still a fancy city lawyer who talks with a plum in his mouth. But Miss McKenzie is no longer a noisy, happy, laughing, colourful, bagpipe-playing girl. She is a quiet lady who has forgotten how to smile using her whole head.

I said that seemed more like take and take. James has *given* nothing and he has *taken* the real Miss McKenzie away.

No give and take.

No real love.

Mum didn't say anything.

She just sighed and became very focused on rinsing the soapsuds down the kitchen sink.

Monday, 12 March

Sam Wotherspoon has the most amazing giant golden squash I have ever seen. He has been picking off every new squash so that the plant puts all its energy into growing the one mega-squash. It's as big as a basketball. Sam is incredibly proud.

Mrs WP was painting the sign at the front gate when we got off the school bus this afternoon.

Our farm used to be called Hillrose Park, but it's been Hillrose POO for over a year now, thanks to Wes and Fez. They changed the sign after a mishap with a flying dead rat and a can of brown paint. Hillrose Poo is a fantastic name for our property. We've never actually had a *park*, but we do have loads of poo — pig poo, chook poo and heaps and heaps of sheep poo.

But today, Clarissa Welsh-Pearson has ruined all that. She's painted the background of the sign totally cream — not a brown blob in sight — and it says Hillrose PARK once again.

Wes and Fez are devastated.

'That was the coolest farm sign in the district, Blue,' Wes cried.

'No-one else had a poo on their sign,' said Fez.

Tonight when Mrs WP complained about Festering Punks screaming out across the plains, Wes and Fez asked if she'd like to listen to Mum's new Beethoven CD. She said yes thank you. So they sent her out to sit on the veranda and played Beethoven.

It took Gertrude about three seconds to leap off Mrs Whittington's veranda at Magpie's Rest, bolt across the driveway, sprint around the corner of the house and head-butt Mrs WP off her chair. Macka appeared from nowhere and gurgled merrily.

Wes and Fez hid in their bedroom and gurgled merrily.

Tuesday, 13 March

Gabby Woodhouse brought her mum's curlers to school today. By home time, every girl in the junior class looked like a poodle. Except for Dora Wilson. You can't curl a crew cut.

Gabby is getting really excited about the wedding and has given Miss McKenzie a folder full of her own hairstyle designs. She still has this mad idea that she will be doing Miss McKenzie's hair on the day!

Mat and Lynette came home with us so we could practise the bridal waltz, ready for the wedding. It was torture. You have to dance with your feet going in this pattern of three beats, but I reckon the odd number just gets everything tangled up.

No matter *how* loudly Mrs WP shouts ONE — TWO — THREE!!! at me, I just can't get it right. Mat and Lynette were dancing like angels drifting around on wispy clouds of joy, while I clomped around like a hippo with a hernia. Petal flew up onto the window sill and pooped in fright.

Dad walked past on his way in for dinner and said, 'Like father, like daughter.'

The last time Dad danced was at the CWA Winter Ball three years ago. In one night, he broke Mum's little toe, knocked over a table full of sandwiches and, somehow, ended up on the floor with Mrs Murphy on top of him.

Wednesday, 14 March

Worms lost his appetite today. He ate half of Lucy Ferris's birthday cake, two egg sandwiches, a muffin and a banana. Then he peeled his orange, looked at it and said, 'I'm full.'

The whole playground went silent.

Everyone was amazed.

Mrs WP tried giving me a private dance lesson this evening. By the time we'd finished, I hadn't improved one bit, and *Mrs WP* was waltzing like a hippo with a hernia.

I thought she'd freak, but when she saw herself in the wardrobe mirror, she burst out laughing.

She laughs like a donkey — really loud and showing lots of teeth. It suits her.

Maybe that's what Sunshine has seen in her — a glimpse of something free.

Mrs WP might be Sunshine's wild donkey.

Uuurk!

Thursday, 15 March

Dreamt that I was being chased by a hippopotamus with a hernia last night. When she finally cornered me, she yelled ONE — TWO — THREE!!! ONE — TWO — THREE!!! ONE — TWO — THREE!!! over and over again. I burst out crying and the hippo sighed heavily and frowned. I woke up in a cold sweat and couldn't go back to sleep.

Mrs WP came to school this morning. She said she wanted to share in some of the charm of Miss McKenzie's country school. Lynette and Matilda Jane greeted her with little squeals and air kisses. Gabby offered her a free hair cut and showed her how cool Dora's hair looks. Worms greeted Mrs WP by throwing up his entire breakfast at her feet — I'm not sure exactly what he'd eaten, but there was lots of it and there were definitely Rice Bubbles and canned peaches involved.

Mrs WP decided that was enough charm for one day. She ran towards the front gate so quickly that she nearly collided with Wes and Fez as they galloped by with tea cosies on their heads, chasing Gary Hartley with a bucket full of compost.

Mr Cluff had a smile from ear to ear. It's the happiest he's looked in ages. He promised to buy Worms a custard tart from the shop at lunch time.

Mrs Whittington was asleep in the grass with Macka, Gunther and the bunnies when we got home. She was hugging a photo of Harold. There was an empty pudding bowl beside Gunther. Darn it! I missed out again!

Friday, 16 March

Mrs WP has gone back to Hathaway Homestead. Mum and Mrs Sweeney took her as far as the Dubbo hospital, where she got a tetanus injection and five stitches in her leg. Mrs WP drove herself the rest of the way home.

Serves her right for trying to kick Gunther and his baby bunnies out of the way just to plant some silly topiary bushes. Topiary is when you trim bushes into perfect shapes instead of letting them do the natural, wild thing. (A bit like stuffing Miss McKenzie's hair into a bun instead of letting it frizz out all over the place.) We now have shrubs shaped like balls, cones, swans and love hearts along the edges of the paved garden paths at Hillrose Poo.

It's a shame Mrs WP's gone, because she might have been interested in the Love Mechanic's letter this week.

Dear Love Mechanic,
There's this really classy sheila who came to my pub the other night. She's from Sydney way and is much better than any of the old bags that live around here.

Should I tell her I think she's a bonzer sheila or is a country bloke like me just dreaming?
Yours sincerely,
Hopeful

The reply was:

Dear Hopeful,
Love is a complicated and beautiful thing. Sometimes you just have to put your heart on the train track of love and risk it being squished by the Wednesday morning freight train from Broken Hill.

You should tell the classy sheila that you love her. Your heart may be totally splattered but, then again, true love may blossom like the roses on a misty morning in spring.

Yours sincerely,
The Love Mechanic

Nice.

Saturday, 17 March

Gertrude has been snorting at the swan-shaped shrubs all day.

Wes and Fez reckon the cone topiary bushes look like Christmas trees and have decorated them with red and white baubles, silver tinsel, little white snowmen and strings of rabbit poo. Just like our tree at Christmas time!

Mrs Whittington is quite upset. She doesn't know how she will organise her wedding to Harold *and* get the Christmas shopping done in time. Miss McKenzie and I spent the afternoon wrapping boxes of tissues and cereal so that Mrs W would have some presents ready. Mum brought a plum pudding and an Advent wreath over to Magpie's Rest at five o'clock and Mrs Whittington finally calmed down. She's out on her front veranda now, listening to 'Angry Orphans in My Attic' by Festering Punks while Gerty, Doris and Mildred eat Christmas dinner by candlelight.

Miss McKenzie is trying on her wedding dress with Mum. I heard her telling Mum about Worms vomiting the other day and they both burst out laughing. It was so good to hear her sparkly laughter again.

Maybe everything will be okay after all.

Sunday, 18 March

Gunther pulled one of the topiary bushes out and offered it to his baby bunnies for lunch. They didn't seem to like it so he pulled out more and more until he realised they preferred grass.

Gerty spent half the day staring at a topiary swan, the hair on her back standing on end. That pig is nuts.

Miss McKenzie spent the afternoon on the internet at our house, hiring one hundred and twenty white chairs and a carpet aisle for the wedding. I suggested she just tell everyone to bring their own chair. Miss McKenzie said she thought that was a lovely idea, but James and Clarissa probably wouldn't like it.

I wanted to shout, 'WHAT ABOUT WHAT *YOU* LIKE???' but I am being very supportive and mature, so I didn't.

Mum and Matilda Jane both would have been so proud of me.

Monday, 19 March

Eight days until Miss McKenzie's mum, dad and little brother, Dougal, arrive from Scotland.

Nine days until Sophie, Peter and Xiu, Peter's best friend, come home.

Ten days until the Easter long weekend begins.

Eleven days until Good Friday.

Which means …

 ONLY
TWELVE DAYS
UNTIL THE
WEDDING!!!

Tuesday, 20 March

Sam Wotherspoon's golden squash is enormous. I don't know how he is even going to lift it when it's time to present it to Miss McKenzie and James.

A group of kids spent lunch time playing weddings. Harry Wilson was the priest and he wore his patchwork hot air balloon as a robe.

Worms and Cassie Ferris were married first. Cassie burst out crying because she wanted to marry Harry and travel to Greenland in his hot air balloon. Then Lynette and Ned Murphy were married. Nick was so upset he ran away and hid behind the toilets for the rest of the day.

Gabby was bawling her eyes out because she didn't get time to do anyone's hair before the weddings, so now they have to do it all over again tomorrow!

Mat has invited me to her place for the weekend. I must have looked scared because she said we could ride Sheba and swim in the dam and I could even bring Petal with me. So I said yes.

Wednesday, 21 March

Gertrude mauled *all* the swan topiary bushes overnight. Don't know what got into her.

Sophie emailed me at school to ask why on *earth* I haven't been keeping her up to date with all the wedding preparations. So I replied during maths, telling her that Wes and Fez have decorated the Christmas trees, the three bridesmaids — Gertrude, Doris and Mildred — are trying to lose weight before Mrs Whittington marries Harold, Sam's giant squash should soon be the size of Russia, Mum has been making plum puddings to feed to the pigs, Dad's harvester has been painted pink to match the rose bushes (once again, Wes and Fez) and I have taught Clarissa Welsh-Pearson to laugh like a donkey and waltz like a hippo with a hernia.

I felt quite cheerful about the whole wedding thing once I'd finished the email. I suppose we really have been having a lot of fun along the way.

I think I just need to keep focusing on the positives.

Thursday, 22 March

Wes married Fez today. When Harry told Wes he could kiss the bride he refused, saying only a sissy pink-pants would kiss his brother. Fez got mad and hit Wes over the head with a zucchini. Wes wrapped Fez up like a sausage roll in Harry's patchwork balloon robe and rolled him all the way across the playground.

Fez was so dizzy when he finally stood up that

he ran into Miss McKenzie and knocked her over. She landed on the edge of the picnic table and broke her nose.

Mat was hysterical and said she hoped Miss McKenzie would look *decent* again by the time the wedding came around. Mr Cluff said Miss McKenzie could have a nose the size of Mount Kosciuszko and cheeks the colour of grass and she would still be beautiful.

Banjo and Mat both thought it was the most romantic thing anyone could ever have said in the whole wide world, but it wasn't. It was just the truth. Anyone who knows and loves Miss McKenzie would agree.

Mr Cluff was really kind and held her in his arms until Mum arrived and took her home. She's been tucked up in bed at Magpie's Rest ever since. Her nose is as wide as mine once more. It looks great. Just like the good old days when she first arrived at Hillrose Poo after being hit in the face by a flying pig-chariot wheel.

We sure are going to miss her.

Friday, 23 March

Miss McKenzie stayed home today, resting in bed with her enormous black and blue nose. Mrs

Whittington watched over her all day, bringing her cups of gravy and teapots full of tomato soup. I think Gerty might have been in to visit too by the look of Miss McKenzie's doona. There was pig snot all over the edges and feathers falling out the end where a hole had been chewed.

I went over after school to show Miss McKenzie my bridesmaid dress, which had been delivered during the day. I was actually surprised at how nice it looked — not too fluffy and frilly at all ... and not even really pink. It's what Mrs WP calls *champagne*. It's what I call *weak tea with milk*.

Miss McKenzie smiled and said I would make the most perfect bridesmaid ever.

Matilda Jane the Mature would be drop-dead jealous if she knew.

Here is today's Love Mechanic letter:

Dear Love Mechanic,
I just marreed a girl at my skool. Duz this meen I hav to shair my food wif her?
From,
Hungree Boy

The Love Mechanic's reply was:

Dear Hungry Boy,

Love is a complicated and beautiful thing. When we love someone we must show that we love them by showering them with beautiful things like red roses, large boxes of expensive chocolates and diamond rings. If you truly love this girl, you will share your chicken salad sandwiches, your mango and peach yoghurt, your shortbread biscuits and your fruit salad. You will even let her sip from your 1 litre cartons of strawberry milk and nibble at your family-size chocolate bars. This might seem painful at first but sometimes, my dear friend, love hurts.

Yours sincerely,

The Love Mechanic

Poor Worms. Love really *will* hurt if he has to give up any of his lunch.

Saturday, 24 March — Sweeney Farm

I'm sitting on Mat's bed writing this while she does my hair. I think she is onto the *fourth* bridesmaid style but that's okay. We've had a great day doing *immature* things like swimming in the dam with Lynette and Petal, building cubbies in the hay bales and making giant chocolate crackles. It's my turn to do something for Mat now.

Mat is beside herself with excitement because James and Miss McKenzie have asked if they can use Sheba to pull the antique buggy for their wedding. I reminded Mat about the gas problem, but she said Sheba is totally cured. According to Mat, Sheba eats only straw and fresh grass and smells like violets and roses.

I seem to remember that Sheba likes to eat anything she can sink her teeth into and then smells like a pit dunny with a dead cow down it.

Never mind. I'm sure Mr Sweeney has it all under control.

Sunday, 25 March

Mat, Lynette and I spent the day helping Mr Sweeney rig up the wedding buggy and harness. It all looks really beautiful — the buggy is shiny and black with cream leather seats. The harness is covered in little bells. There is a headdress for the horse that looks a bit like a silver volcano with fluffy white feathers spouting out the top.

Sheba seemed quite proud of herself when she was all fitted out, and trotted around the driveway like a circus pony, even though she's twice the size of a normal horse.

Mat was so pleased and excited, I don't think she even noticed the bad smells that were drifting around.

I just hope there's a fresh breeze blowing across the plains next Saturday ...

Monday, 26 March

Miss McKenzie was back at school today, but she was pretty quiet. I think her nose must still be throbbing. It has turned a lovely bruised rainbow of yellow, purple and green. It's a shame there's no pink to match the bridesmaid dresses and the harvester.

Wes and Fez have special crew cuts for the wedding! They came home with nits and before Mum could treat them with chemicals, Mrs Whittington had shaved their heads. After all, that's what they used to do when she was a girl.

Mum was horrified. She said Wes and Fez would look like little criminals for the wedding. I said they *are* little criminals and it's time we told everyone the truth.

Wes and Fez said it would all be fine because Mrs Whittington was going to knit them new tea cosies for the big day.

Mum sighed and went into her room for a little lie-down.

Tuesday, 27 March

Miss McKenzie's family are here at Hillrose Poo and they are just lovely.

Her dad, Angus, is tall and chunky and has red hair and a bushy beard. His eyes twinkle just like Miss McKenzie's used to, and he laughs all the time. Her mum, Glenda, is small and quiet but her eyes still twinkle and she never stops smiling.

Miss McKenzie's brother, Dougal, is ten and has red hair and freckles. He's as crazy as Wes and Fez and has already crashed a pig chariot, learnt to do flips off the trampoline, juggled four dead mice at once and got Macka to spit on him. Wes and Fez reckon he's the most awesome friend to have visited since Xiu came last Easter with a suitcase full of firecrackers.

At dinner tonight, Dad and Angus had an arm wrestle and Angus shoved Dad's hand down into the trifle. Glenda scraped the jelly off Dad's hand with a teaspoon and ate it, laughing all the time. They were interested in everyone and everything, and didn't seem to think it was odd that Mrs Whittington wore her wedding dress to dinner, or that we played a song called 'Ugly, Ugly, Ugly World' five times after dessert.

They are so perfect. Just like Miss McKenzie.

I wonder how they will get on with the Welsh-Pearsons …

Wednesday, 28 March

They're home. Sophie and Peter are back at Hillrose Poo where they belong. Xiu is here for Easter too.

Dad drove them through Hardbake Plains so they could call in at school before they went home. Sophie and Mat squealed like a pair of cockatoos when they saw each other. They air kissed and did the whole bridesmaid thing where they talked about their dresses, hairstyles, bouquets and a whole heap of other stuff I didn't even understand. Then they did it all over again when Sophie saw Miss McKenzie. It was exhausting.

Mr Cluff must have found it exhausting too, because he sat on the veranda with his head in his hands, sighing.

Harry Wilson asked Xiu if he'd like a wedding and, before Xiu knew what had hit him, he and Mat were married beside Lucy's rabbit hutch. When Harry told Xiu he could kiss the bride, Mat lunged forward and kissed Xiu ON THE LIPS!!!

All the big kids rolled around laughing themselves stupid. The little kids thought it was disgusting and yelled out stuff like EW, URK, YUCKY, POO.

Mat was so embarrassed that she burst into tears, pushed Harry over and ran into the girls' toilets to hide. Sophie ran after her.

What will Warren from Warren say when he finds out?

Thursday, 29 March

Such a sad, sad day.

And not even having Sophie and Peter at home can make it feel better.

Had a sausage sizzle at lunch time to farewell Miss McKenzie from Hardbake Plains Public School FOREVER.

The McKenzies came to school to share in the special farewell. They loved all the animals and Sam's vegie patch. Glenda told Harry that

184

his hot air balloon looked just splendid and that he was welcome to stay with them at Dingwall if ever he flew over Scotland. Angus let Gabby comb and style his beard and pretended to be quite happy with the ribbons she tied all through it.

After lunch we had an Easter egg hunt and Angus got stuck under the tank stand when he was searching for eggs for Dora and Cassie. Wes and Fez said they could chop his arms and legs off, because that's what the famous contortionist Vincent Van Gogh did every time he got stuck somewhere awkward. But Mr Cluff wouldn't let them. Miss McKenzie finally crawled under the other side and shoved him out.

Just before home time, Mr Cluff gave a farewell speech. He said Miss McKenzie was the best thing ever to have happened to Hardbake Plains. She had brought joy and light and fun and love to our school, and the Bake will be a poorer place when she is gone.

Everyone was crying by the end. Gary Hartley and Nick Farrel were blubbering so much they couldn't even perform the special Highland fling they had been rehearsing all term. Worms cried so hard he threw up. Although it could also have been because of the seventeen Easter eggs he'd just eaten.

So the day ended on a bit of a low, I suppose. Everyone walked out through the front gate as though they were leaving a funeral. Even Miss McKenzie and her mum and dad.

Mr Cluff was left all alone, standing at the gate, looking like a maggoty dead sheep had just slammed full pelt into his life.

Friday, 30 March — Good Friday

Only one sleep to go!

Woke up with a sinking feeling in my tummy. Ate three hot cross buns for breakfast, which made the sinking feeling even worse.

The whole place was CRAZY all day, with trucks and armies of people coming and going. There were big white tents and rows of seats popping up all over the yard. We have thousands of fairy lights strung up in the trees and dozens of chefs in white hats shooing Mum from the kitchen. As if Mum's sausage rolls and lamingtons aren't good enough!

All this fuss over one little wedding.

James, Mrs Welsh-Pearson and Alex arrived before lunch. Alex is the best man, although I can't see what makes him any better than Dad or Mr Cluff or any of the other blokes around here.

Mrs WP was horrified when she saw the garden. The bushes Wes and Fez have decorated as Christmas trees looked so bright and festive, you'd hardly notice the mauled swans or the uprooted balls and hearts. But Mrs WP wants everything to be *perfect* for the wedding. She made Peter and Xiu pull *all* the bushes out and burn them behind the shed. What a waste!

Mrs Whittington was quite distressed about the Christmas trees vanishing this close to 25 December. Wes and Fez were quite distressed that their strings of rabbit poo had been so thoughtlessly destroyed. First the poo on the farm sign, now the poo on the trees ... If I was Mrs WP, I wouldn't be messing with Wes and Fez like this. They are still quite emotional about not being included as bridesmaids.

Had a rehearsal of the wedding ceremony before dinner. It all seemed to go okay, except for the part where Miss McKenzie said *I* was the chief bridesmaid and had to hold her bouquet. Mat was livid because she thought *she* was the most important bridesmaid on earth. She stormed off in a huff, tripped over the edge of the carpet aisle and landed face first on the back of a chair. Her bottom lip is now looking unattractively large. Her brain, however, is obviously still attractively small. I tried to console her by pointing this out but she just burst into tears and said some quite hurtful things about my red hair and dancing talents.

Anyway, Princess Mat and Lynette have gone home now and the Welsh-Pearsons are at the pub for dinner, so at last things are back to normal here. Sophie is piercing her bellybutton with a safety pin. The boys are playing Truth or Dare and Peter is running around the back yard in Mum's nighty with grapes stuck up his nose. Mrs Whittington is digging up a new vegie patch in front of the seating for the wedding. She has turned all the fairy lights on so she can see in the dark. 'Angry Orphans in My Attic' by Festering Punks is blasting out across the plains.

Saturday, 31 March — The Wedding
2.45 pm

I am sitting at the dining table writing this. The moment I was all dressed and decorated as a bridesmaid, Mum plonked me down with a novel, my diary and a pen and has forbidden me to move an inch. I think she's scared I'll tear my dress or fall over and get grass stains. At least I have a great view of the back yard from here.

I feel stupid as. The dress is okay. It's all the other stuff I hate. My shoes have high heels and I'm limping before I even *start* the bridesmaid's walk up that long carpet aisle. I have pink lipstick on, which makes me feel like I've eaten a sticky bun and not had time to wipe my mouth clean. My hair looks like something Gabby Woodhouse has designed — all puffed up, with flowers and corkscrews dangling in odd places. It's *really* embarrassing.

The pigs and Macka are locked away in the shearing shed yard. Wes and Fez are in their little black suits and ties. The food and champagne is set up in the big white tent at the end of the yard and I can just see the enormous wedding cake on its special table under the peppercorn tree.

Miss McKenzie is getting dressed at Magpie's Rest. At 4 o'clock we'll all be picked up at Mrs Whittington's front veranda in the buggy — Angus, Miss McKenzie, Mat, Sophie, Lynette and me. We'll be driven around the house to the back yard, where everyone will be waiting in their seats for Miss McKenzie to walk down the aisle and marry James Welsh-Pearson.

I must be happy for Miss McKenzie's sake.

I must be happy for Miss McKenzie's sake.

I must be happy for Miss McKenzie's sake.

3.10 pm

Mum has just brought Petal in to me. She found her swimming around in the punch bowl, bobbing between the bits of floating fruit and ice. The chefs weren't very happy.

3.20 pm

Good grief!

Sheba has escaped and is outside the dining-room window eating the rosemary bushes. Her feather headdress is bobbing up and down excitedly. She must be getting into a real feeding frenzy.

I know she shouldn't eat anything other than fresh grass or oats, but I can't go outside and stop her. Mum has promised to kill me and bury me behind the chook shed if I move a millimetre from the dining table. I just have to sit here and watch.

Hope the wedding is over before Sheba starts digesting too much ...

3.35 pm

Mr Sweeney laughed his socks off when he found Sheba. I could be wrong, but I reckon he patted her neck and told her she was a good girl as he led her away.

Uh-oh! Worms has just disappeared into the big white tent for his own feeding frenzy ...

3.40 pm

Sam Wotherspoon has presented his wedding gift to James. The giant squash is so big he had to carry it in a wheelbarrow. Unfortunately it tipped over at the last minute and the squash lived up to its name — it *squashed* James's foot.

I can just see him limping over to the wedding area now. I don't think he even said thank you to Sam.

How rude is that?

3.50 pm

Oh no. Here comes Mum. I think I am about to be the most embarrassing bridesmaid on Earth …

11.45 pm

Miss McKenzie has left Hillrose Poo.

She is gone.

I am devastated.

At 4 o'clock Sheba pulled up beside Magpie's Rest and took Mrs Whittington to the wedding. She wore her old wedding dress with the yellow hem and the torn sleeves, and had geranium flowers in her hair. She looked lovely and very happy.

Of course, Miss McKenzie and us bridesmaids were meant to go to the wedding in the buggy, but Mrs Whittington got confused and thought it was for her. It was kinder to just let her go.

We ended up travelling to the back yard in the pink harvester with Dad. Miss McKenzie laughed her head off, and said it was the best way ever to go to her wedding. She was really glad I'd brought Petal along too. She said it gave that extra country touch to the whole celebration. It was the happiest she's been in weeks.

Five hideous bagpipes screeched the Bridal March, and we walked down the aisle — Sophie,

Mat, Lynette, then Petal and me. Matilda Jane the Mature was so busy fluttering her eyelashes at Xiu that she ran into Sophie and they both tripped over. I limped all the way, and Petal limped along beside me. Honest to goodness I tried not to, for Miss McKenzie's sake. But that step-drag-ankles-together thing combined with the high-heeled shoes was a recipe for disaster. James glared at me all the way. He probably thought I was mocking his own limp from Sam's squash, but I just couldn't help it.

Finally Miss McKenzie tip-toed along the carpet aisle. She held onto Angus's arm like she was scared of drowning or falling over a cliff.

Just as she reached James, the bagpipes began a new tune. A putrid smell, fresh from Sheba's dodgy digestive system, filled the air and everything went haywire all at once.

Mrs Whittington leapt up from her seat and started sobbing that Miss McKenzie was stealing her husband. Gabby Woodhouse leapt up from her seat and started sobbing that no-one appreciated her talent as a hairdresser. Gavin O'Donnell *stood* up on his seat and yelled that he loved Matilda Jane even though she smelt like a pit dunny on a hot night after a busy day.

Gertrude appeared from around the corner of the house and charged up the aisle, straight towards James and Miss McKenzie. The sound of the bagpipes had drifted across the plains to the sheep yards, driving her nuts. She must have head-butted the gate until it smashed open and the pigs and Macka were free.

The bagpipers played on and Gerty squealed in fury. She bared her teeth and lunged at James. James grabbed Miss McKenzie and pushed her in front of himself as a HUMAN SHIELD!!! So much for that *greater love has no man* stuff ...

Miss McKenzie was head-butted sideways, straight into the grass near Gunther and his bunnies. Gunther was furious. He bared his teeth and leapt on Miss McKenzie's frothy white dress, tearing it into hundreds of tiny shreds.

At the same moment we heard Wes and Fez shout, 'Five, four, three, two, one, blast off!'

Dougal was launched from the Flying Ferals' best catapult ever. He flew through the air, his kilt flapping heroically, until he landed head first in the wedding cake.

Wes and Fez ran after him cheering and yelling, 'Happy wedding, Miss McKenzie!'

They were wearing Incredible Hulk undies over their black wedding suits and pink tea cosies on their heads. Mrs WP would have been very glad to see that they had tried to match the roses and the harvester.

Mildred sprinted to the cake and started vacuuming it up as quickly as she could. Doris knocked Dougal to the ground and licked the icing from his face.

Miss McKenzie stood up with her skirt in tatters, her pink and orange striped knickers showing underneath. Her red hair had escaped its bun and was frizzing out all over the place. Her make-up had rubbed off on the grass and she had dirt smeared down one cheek. She was totally freckled and feral and her eyes were twinkling like they used to in the good old days before James Welsh-Pearson came along and ruined everything.

Miss McKenzie looked over at Dougal and the squashed cake. Fez smiled at her through his bug-eyed glasses and false teeth, and Wes gave her the thumbs up.

She burst out laughing and staggered around like a maniac. She laughed so hard she snorted a bit of dirt out her nose and that made her laugh even more.

Mrs Welsh-Pearson looked like she was about to faint.

James limped forward and shouted, 'Katherine! Behave! Pull yourself together!'

Mr Cluff jumped out of his seat and yelled, 'Don't talk like that to the woman I love!'

Mr Cluff seemed to inspire Sunshine, because *he* jumped up and yelled, 'I love you, Clarissa!'

Dad cried, 'Her name's Jacinta!'

James shouted, 'Jacinta's a cow!!!'

And Dad said, 'That's no way to talk about your mother!'

Miss McKenzie burst into a fresh round of laughter. She plonked down onto the grass beside Dougal and pulled her veil and shoes off.

I think that's when James realised it was over.

WHAT A RELIEF!

James and Mrs Welsh-Pearson were furious. James was snarling like Gunther when he tries to protect his babies. Only James was just protecting himself.

They were stomping across the garden to leave, when Worms came out of the food tent, holding his tight little belly and moaning. He staggered over to Mrs WP, burped and threw up all over her shoes. Macka appeared from nowhere and trotted around gurgling happily.

The Welsh-Pearsons drove away followed closely by their guests, and I *thought* we would all live happily ever after.

It's never that easy with love, though, is it?

Miss McKenzie stood up in front of the Bake crowd and said, 'I think I'll go home for a while.'

And by the way she looked at Glenda and Angus, we knew that she didn't mean Magpie's Rest. She meant Scotland.

So she left.

Just like that.

She got in the car with Glenda, Angus and Dougal and drove away — down the driveway, through the front gate and away from Hillrose Poo.

Out of our lives.

April

Sunday, 1 April — Easter Sunday

The McKenzies rang from Sydney just before their flight left today. They thanked us for all we had done, wished us a happy Easter and promised to keep in touch.

Miss McKenzie said she *will* be back. She just needs a break to sort herself out.

She probably needs a break for all Gunther's tooth marks to heal.

I don't want to sound like Matilda Jane the Love Mechanic, but she probably needs a break for her heart to heal too.

Love is a complicated and ugly thing. Sometimes it is shallow and fading, like Matilda Jane's love for Gavin, and Banjo's love for me. Sometimes it is bossy and cold and not really there at all, like James's love for Miss McKenzie. People call this love, but I think they have given it the wrong name.

But now I'm beginning to understand that love can also be a complicated and *beautiful* thing.

When Mum loves Dad even though he wears his muddy boots in the house, and Dad loves Mum even though he hates her taste in music, that is love.

When Gunther adores his ducklings and his bunnies as though they are perfect little piglets, that is love.

When Fez loves Wes even though he won't kiss him in public, that is love.

When Mrs Whittington still falls asleep clutching a photo of Harold to her chest nine years after he has died, that is love.

When Petal nibbles my cheeks and follows me around, that is love.

When Nick still wants to have *I love Lynette's guts* tattooed on his shoulder, even after Lynette has married Ned Murphy, that is love.

When you still want to be with someone, despite the fact that they play the bagpipes, laugh at maggot-infested sheep, snort chocolate mousse out their nose, let their carroty hair frizz out like saltbush in the wind and have desperately feral friends, that is true love. Just ask Mr Cluff.

True love accepts people as they are, even if there are a few hiccups and shocks along the way.

I don't know much about love, but I do know that.

Look out for Blue's next adventure!

Turn the page for a sneak peek …

Monday, 16 April — Start of Term 2

Today is a very important day in the history of Hardbake Plains. I am so excited!

Mat, Ben and I are starting a newspaper for our big year seven English project. Hardbake Plains has never had a newspaper before. Not even when the population grew to 237 people during the wool boom of the 1800s.

At first Matilda Jane the Mature wasn't going to help. She really wanted us all to create a fashion magazine called *Matilda's Wardrobe*. But then Ben sat on her for one and a half hours and she kindly agreed to do the newspaper instead.

We have already decided that it will be called *The Bake Tribune*. Other papers have grand names like *The Herald*, *The Chronicle* and *The Proclaimer*, so we reckon Hardbake Plains' first-ever newspaper should have a special name.

The Bake Tribune
THE BAKE TRIBUNE
The bake tribune

However you write it, it looks terribly important. It's bound to be a success.

Tuesday, 17 April

Our new teacher is arriving on Friday.

The school has had a lot of trouble getting someone to take Miss McKenzie's place while she's in Scotland. Everyone's saying it's because we are so far out west and such a tiny town. But I know it's because people are scared of Wes and Fez. Everyone here is used to them — a bit like people who live in the Swiss Alps are used to avalanches, or people in Kenya are used to lions. But to the outsider, Wes and Fez would seem terrifying, dangerous and strange.

Mr Cluff doesn't make the place look so good either. He's been such a gloomy guts since Miss McKenzie left. He mopes around like a zombie with a toothache. Not a welcoming sight.

I really thought Miss McKenzie would be back by the start of the new term, but she hasn't even mentioned coming home. She might be Scottish by birth, but she really does belong here at Hardbake Plains. She fitted in from the day she arrived. As Dad said, Miss McKenzie became as Aussie as a cockatoo eating a lamington in a gumtree.

We had our first executive meeting for *The Bake Tribune* today. Hopefully the first edition will be out in a few weeks. I am going to be the editor and chief reporter. Ben will be the designer and printer. Mat is having trouble deciding on what she wants to contribute, because she is an expert in *so* many areas — fashion, romance, skin care, romance, diets, romance, boarding school, romance … I suppose she'll sort it out sooner or later.

My duck Petal will have to be chief editor's paperweight. She has started coming to school with me again. Mrs Whittington tried to bake her for an early Christmas dinner last week, so I don't really feel like she is safe at home without me.

Wednesday, 18 April

Mat has decided that she will write a romance serial for *The Bake Tribune*. She is not quite sure what to call it yet, but it's certain to be something totally embarrassing, like *Safari into Love* or *Colliding Hearts*.

She said her trip to the Dubbo Zoo in the school holidays with Warren from Warren has given her plenty of ideas for the love scenes (smirk, blush, giggle …). Apparently she had a million romantic experiences in a single day. Warren grasped her hand every time they were near the tigers (I think that shows he's a big, fat scaredy pants, but Mat assures me it's a sign of deep affection). He gazed into her eyes *five times* near the camels, and kissed her cheek behind the elephants.

Ben was busy doing an online maths challenge and thought Mat said Warren had kissed the cheek of an elephant's behind. Ben has always thought Warren from Warren sounded like a real nerd, but now he's not so sure. Anyone brave enough to kiss an elephant on the butt has Ben's total respect and admiration.

Two days until the new teacher arrives …

About the author

Katrina Nannestad grew up in central west New South Wales. After studying arts and education at the University of New England in Armidale, she worked as a primary school teacher. Her first teaching job was at a tiny two-teacher school in the bush. Katrina now lives near Bendigo with her husband, two sons and a pea-brained whippet.